ON MY BEING DEAD AND OTHER STORIES

ON MY BEING DEAD AND OTHER STORIES

L.W. Michaelson

Published by The Galileo Press Baltimore 1983

Grateful acknowledgement is made to the editors of the publications in which the following stories first appeared:

"The Burglar Face," *Kansas Quarterly;* "An Early Frost" and "All My Darlings," *Descant;* "The Ferrari," *Prairie Schooner,* reprinted in *Best Articles & Stories;* "The Goldfish," *Ramparts;* "The Burning Bush," *Mutiny,* reprinted in *Short Story International;* "The Flying Dutchman," *Parnassus;* "The Rabbit That Lost Its Nose" and "The Concert-Goer," *North American Review;* "Klitzee One—God Zero," *Mississippi Review;* "Butcherdom"; "Me and Will" and "Phocian", *Samsidat;* "The Rhyme in Freddy's Face," *Wind.*

Cover Art by John J. Sorbie

ISBN 0-913123-02-1

Library of Congress Catalog Card Number 83-81251
All Rights Reserved

98765432
First Edition

Published by The Galileo Press, Post Office Box 16129, Baltimore, Maryland.

Other Books by L.W. Michaelson

Songs of My Divided Self (South & West Inc., Publishers)
New Shoes on an Old Man (Pierian Springs Press)
Everyone Revisited (Prairie Gate Press)

To my wife Annie, and to my late
ex-teacher, Vincent McHugh

CONTENTS

THE BURGLAR FACE

"But it is whining again," he said, "and it is scratching the door, and I have just painted it again, and I have warned you..."

The wife rolled over in bed and pulled a pillow over her head and her muffled voice came: "If you don't pay any attention, it will stop whining... pretty soon."

"But that's not the point," the husband said, his voice grating through her feather barrier, "I agreed to buy a dog on the one condition we use it to train the children into responsibility; I..."

"Please! Not at three a.m. in the morning! No lectures now. I will let the dog out."

"Fine thing!" the husband sputtered.

She got out of bed, her breasts heaving behind the flimsy barrier of her nightgown, her long dark hair sweeping the bed clothes, and stood on the bare floor beside the bed groping for her wrapper.

"Fine thing!" the husband went on. "The damn dog trains you!" And then he spread out luxuriously on the soft white bed while his wife went slop slop in her slippers and let the dog out, a whiny German pointer with red-rimmed yellow eyes, and while she waited for the dog to finish his business, the wind took her wrapper and she spread her arms out to the August moon floating high above, and she whispered a curse against all husbands, and the clouds swept past the moon and there was a sudden chill in the sodden air, and the dog came back quickly at her call, and she slopped back in her slippers to the bedroom, holding her arms to her breasts to keep warm.

She crept inside the covers then, hoping to soothe the husband with her body, but he would have none of her and turned from her, and so she tossed all the night long.

They began again at breakfast. "Well, stupid," he said. "Dog lover!" And then he banged the coffeepot down on the polished table. "Dog lovers of the world unite! You've nothing to lose but your sleep, you've nothing to lose but your hus—"

"But he's a good dog," the wife interrupted. "He's young yet and his bowels are weak. Besides, some night a burglar will come and... "

"Bah!" the husband snorted. "I will take a nice, clean, orderly burglar any day to Sambo who craps on the floor, who whines, who wants in, who wants out! And what's more is guilty of the most unforgivable crime for a hunting dog—gun shy!"

"We have always had a dog in our house! Always! Always!" she said, and her voice began to rise in pitch, although she had not intended it so. "It is you, not the dog, that is the trouble!"

"Bah!" he answered, and went from the house in a rage, grinding the gears of their new car as he sped out the driveway in anger.

And so it went, week after week, night after night, for the dog was now in the habit of going out in the middle of the night, and sometimes, in a frenzy, the husband would jerk a child from its bed, and drag it down the stairs to take care of the dog, and the child would cry hysterically not knowing quite what had happened, feeling perhaps that some giant had seized it in the dark, and the wife would follow the husband and the bewildered child down the stairs and out into the cool night air, crying softly: "No, no... I will take the dog out."

And the wife thought at these times if only she could prove to him that every house far in the country should have a dog, *must* have a dog for protection against prowlers and tramps, and finally the thought came to her, sitting one morning over breakfast, that she would hire a burglar, a fake burglar, to stage a robbery in the night and the dog, Sambo, would bark, and then her husband would see he was worth his dog food and all would be right again with their marriage. But then as she sat at the table, stirring her coffee, after the husband had gone to work, she wondered if she was telling herself the truth about the dog; her need for the dog was, well, perhaps nostalgia for her youth: she needed to hold onto it, to remember her old home in the far country, and her mother, and how they always had hunting dogs, and Sambo stood for her past somehow... but no, not quite. What was it? Dogs teach children love and affection, true enough—yet, in truth, Toby and Marse never paid much attention to Sambo. Perhaps she was recreating a dead past for her children, and the dog would be a landmark, a peg to hang memories on.

She put these random thoughts from her mind and forced herself to think about the burglar. How did one hire a thief? It was all too fantastic. One couldn't go to the journals and advertise. What did one do? Sit in some shady tavern and look for the right face, a burglar face? No, she could not do it.

But then, one night soon after a particularly painful scene about the dog, she and her husband had gone to a neighborhood party. Claus, her husband's best friend was there and he had more than a little to drink, and as usual he began a mild flirtation with her as he always did, mainly to flatter the husband, and the wife winked back, something she had not done before. And so in a little while, Claus danced her behind a doorway for a little kiss, and he said then: "My, that was nice. Are there any more someplace?" And she laughed and said, "Naughty," and then on impulse she whispered in his ear: "But there just might be, *someplace*. But you must pay for them!"

And Claus was immediately intrigued, and pushed her against the door and ran his hands over her body quickly before she could pull away. "Yes?" he said, and before the party was over they had arranged a rendezvous for the next day.

It was over tea, at a little shop above a dry goods store in the village, they had met and she told him softly of her troubles with the dog and her plans about the burglar. And Claus had laughed aloud, causing people to stare at them, and he said:"Oh, you are a silly, silly child! I can't take you seriously. Besides," he went on looking at her with his red-streaked eyes, "this all shows you love your husband very, very much to want to teach the clod a lesson, and I will have no part in this . . . no part in reviving fading love affairs between husband and wife. It all has to do with Freud . . . or . . . impotency, anyway." And then he gave her a saucy wink and clutched her hand atop the table and said, "I had hoped . . . well, you know what I had hoped."

And then, on impulse, the wife rolled her eyes at him and sighed in a very special way that she used sometimes at the climax of the sex act, and began to stroke the palm of his hand that was clutching hers in a sensuous fashion, and she did not draw away when, suddenly, Claus slid his other hand on her leg under the table, and thus Claus became intrigued once again, and said, "We will talk of this plan some more soon, a little more privately, eh?"

And he left her at the tea shop with this promise of more trouble to come, and the wife was terribly confused for this was not how she planned things at all, and maybe, she thought then, it would be best to sell the dog, or even shoot it with her husband's shotgun and not get involved with this man, Claus, for he was a sticky fellow, indeed, and she could sense he would not be gotten rid of after the burglary—if there was to be one at all.

Three nights later, her husband had gone to an evening meeting of his hunting club, and she had put the children, Marse and Toby, to bed, and she was sitting over her meal with an after-dinner brandy, and the gentle, hot fingers of the brandy warmed her stomach and seemed to curl about her very womb. And as she sat, she petted the dog, Sambo, who was whining softly to go out and looking up at her with his hideous yellow and red-rimmed eyes, and slobbering a good deal on her sleeve, when the phone rang and it was Claus and he said that he had been thinking it over (although on the phone it had sounded to the wife as if he had been *drinking* it over), and that it now seemed a fairly reasonable thing to do, "to help a lady in distress" (although, again, on the phone it had sounded more like "help a lady out of her dress"), but that if he were to burgle the house he must come over soon and *look her things over,* and "wasn't her husband at the lodge meeting?" he asked, and went on saying that he didn't want to wander around in the dark at her house and "trip and fall over her things" and not know just how and when and where to force entry, and he wanted to talk on and on. "Stop!" said the wife, for she belatedly got the drift that he was not talking about the house at all, and a warm, red flush spread across her face, and it felt, for a minute, as if she had been drinking brandy. "I mean," she said, "this is a party line." And she was a bit worried, although it was pretty late in the evening for local farm folk to be up and eavesdropping on the line, so she whispered in her poor French for him to come over at once and she would show him the house and grounds, and he said *tout a coup,* and she put the phone down with a large sigh, and the dog, Sambo, came over and whined to be let out.

It was a daring thing to do, to ask him over, for she didn't quite know how long her husband would be at the lodge, but she knew she must get this affair over with soon, for their quarrels about the dog had been getting more and more intense, and she was getting less sleep at nights for fear the dog would whine and provoke another early morning scene, and thus she had been keeping awake half the night to anticipate the dog's needs before whining aroused the husband.

So, in less than half an hour there was Claus at the door and he had a half-filled bottle of brandy in his hand, and while she led the way, he looked the house over and tried the French doors that led out to the terrace, but the wife said then in exasperation, "But Claus, you've been here many times, and you must know our house well enough!"

"But not like a burglar knows a house, dear," he had answered, "and if your husband comes home suddenly, I will be here to borrow his golf clubs, so it will be all right."

Thus, reluctantly, she led him on a tour of the downstairs, and he saw where Sambo slept at night near the French doors, and she flung wide the doors and they went out onto the terrace, and as she had opened the doors she had the strangest feeling that she was undressing before him, and the doors were the sides of her sheer dressing gown that she had opened. He had pushed past her rudely, flourishing the brandy bottle, and began to explain to her the route he would take. "I will drive up here," he said, pointing the brandy bottle at the dark, "feeling a perfect ass all the while, with my lights out, and my head swimming; then, I will cross the rose garden and with some heavy hunting boots on, trampling down the flowers, so I will leave tracks for the police...and...ah...the husband. And then I will come up upon this terrace!"

He said this last triumphantly and the wife had shivered slightly, and Claus took her by the hand and led her down through the rose garden, heavy with scent, and back again onto the terrace as he spoke. "And I will force entrance *here!*" And as he stood by the French doors, toying with the doorknob, he reached for her quickly, and the wife was so confused she, for the first time in her life, could find no words or movements to stop the advances of a male.

And there was moonlight on the terrace, and soft, Indian-summer winds, and his hands began to caress her as if they were separate entities detached from any body or will, and he pressed her gently down upon the settee that her husband was fond of sleeping upon in the summer, and somehow, there, with the dog, Sambo, whining softly in the background, he possessed her quickly and efficiently, and she knew then as she strained against him, almost against her will, that her husband's house, in truth, had been burgled and it was too late to cry out for Sambo to bark a warning.

Then, a brief while later, at an awkward pause in their love-making, she had said to Claus: "Well, in spite of this I must teach him a lesson about the dog, you and I, I mean," and then she ran her smooth hands on his strong young legs that were naked in the moonlighht. "Let us run away," Claus had said then, "run away from dogs and husbands," and in the night his voice had sounded almost sincere.

"No, you and I are not going to get married," she said in reply. "I have a comfortable house. Two children who would never adjust to you and your bachelor ways. Things are just the same, only we must teach him a lesson about the dog."

"Oh, you females!" Claus said. "Who has been talking about marriage! I have been talking about flight." And at this he disengaged himself from her limbs and got up to go, but the wife pulled him down to her again upon the settee, and said: "Claus! You promised about the dog!"

"But your husband is such a hunter—a crack shot! He has guns . . . guns for every occasion!" And he pointed his brandy bottle (that he somehow had clutched all the time upon the settee) to the guns that hung on the walls of the living room just inside. "And if he awakes too soon and starts to shoot like at a trap meet? What then, my pretty one?" And at that he began to pour brandy on Sambo, who had come too close to them, sniffling and snuffling, and then, laughing outrageously, he poured brandy on the wife's bare breasts, stark white in the light of the fall moon.

"Oh, stop!" she said in irritation, and took her white slip lying on the terrace floor and wiped her skin dry while Claus sniggered at her and drank deeply from the bottle. "It was a christening," he said. "The breasts that launched a thousand . . . a thousand . . . brandy bottles!"

"Be quiet!" she said and began to talk nervously about the robbery. "The point is, not to be afraid. Sambo is sure to bark long before any real trouble. You quickly break the glass in the French doors, knock over a vase or two, and then run for your car, and that is all."

They had parted after that and the husband came home shortly after and made violent love to her and there was no trouble about the dog for the weather was Indian-summer warm, and Sambo slept soundly all the night long on the terrace curled up on the settee, but the husband did stop, once, at his love-making and ask if she had been drinking wine.

The next week Claus called again on the phone and speaking in French had insisted upon a rendezvous at a cheap motel outside the village, a meeting that had quickly and perfunctorily ended in her submission once again, and he still seemed vague about his part in the robbery, but she had said to him at the motel door when they parted, "But I will pay you money, much money," for she knew now that her body was not enough for him. But he had said only, "Perhaps,"and she went home sadly, not knowing if Claus would ever play his part.

But it wasn't too long after that, the lover, Claus, got a whispered phone call in the night. "Things look right," the wife said with her heart in her throat, for she did not know how Claus would respond. "He has gone to bed early. The dog is sleeping by the French doors, and there is a vase handy, and...I..."

"*Oui, ma chérie. Tout a coup,*" Claus had whispered on sudden impulse, for he had grown to need her, and then he said something quite indecent to her, again in French, about her skill in bed, and a warm flush spread over her face, and then she said, "*Oui. Tout a coup,*" and then she hung up the phone with a strange, ecstatic smile on her face, and returned to her husband's bed. He was awake, sitting bolt upright in bed, with a queer, twisted smile that the wife had never seen before. "Were you on the phone at this late hour?" he asked.

"I...I...think the children left it off the hook. It was making a strange noise. I talked to the operator."

"Oh," he said. Then he reached over to the end table, got a book, and began to read. "I will read a bit. You go to sleep."

She watched him for a while. She wondered if she should make love to him so he would sleep, but then she thought it would be just as well if he was awake and heard the dog barking. In a minute or two she went sound asleep for both her lover and her husband had been sexually demanding of late, and thus she slept deeply.

But then, from far off, she heard a great noise. And it came louder, and again, and she heard the dog, Sambo, send up a terrible, terrible howling, and then there was a sudden, monstrous, pregnant stillness in the house, and she got out of bed, her breasts heaving like the sea against the flimsy barrier of her nightdress, and she walked barefoot as one in a trance down to the room leading to the terrace, murmuring, crooning to herself, "The children, the children,"and there was no light in the rooms downstairs, but the late autumn moon bathed the room and the terrace in a cold, dim light, and the first thing she saw was a great deal of blood, spattered against the French doors, and she turned her head downward with a great effort, but then quickly closed her eyes in pain, for the dog, Sambo, lay dead upon the floor of the room. As she knelt slowly down on the floor in kind of a stupor, her fingers trailing in the dog's warm blood, she could hear her husband's voice come floating to her as from far across a body of water: "You see," the husband said. "The fool dog didn't bark at all. He loves everybody . . . *even burglars!*"

And she started to speak, "But it isn't true, none of it!" The words formed on her lips but no sound came forth. Then the husband stepped across the body of the dog and made a quick motion with his hand, and the lights were on now, brilliant, boring into the wife's skull, and she knew the softness and kindness of her world, a special world made for dogs and children alone had faded forever, and as she was about to sink down into a faint, she wanted to scream at her husband to keep the children out of the room if they should come down, but her husband grasped her roughly by the shoulders and shook her. "You listen to me!" he said. And she saw her husband make a strange grimace; his eyes shifted quickly, back and forth, and she heard his voice rasping: "There was a man . . . a *burglar*. Ah, he didn't get anything of . . . ah . . . value, I trust. I think I hit him with some light bird shot, and Sambo got in the way. The burglar got away, though. Drove away in a rather expensive car, I do believe. Business must be good."

"Well?" she said listlessly.

"Well! Well, shall we get still *another* dog, *ma cherie?*"

Two days later she went to see Claus. Highly indignant, Claus had ordered her to dig No. 8 bird shot from his thighs and posterior, for he had not dared see a doctor, and the wounds, though very slight, were festering. In the middle of her ministrations, the wife began to snicker. Later, when Claus attempted to make love to her, she laughed hysterically, and he ended his advances abruptly. "This...this is the gratitude I get! Laughter! I might have been killed! And for what!"

"Sambo is dead," she said. "Will you...will you get me another dog?"

"You have me instead," he said, and he reached for her again, tenderly, and this time she did not pull away or laugh.

Later, as she dressed before him, putting on her things slowly, the way he liked her to, and then finally standing at the doorway with her blouse unbuttoned to her navel, and her brassiere left lying on the floor, she waved goodbye to Claus, and she smiled happily. "Ah...ah...aren't you forgetting something," he asked, and pointed to the floor.

"No, it's done deliberately. So he will wonder a bit." And then she said: "You know, a dog or a lover somehow puts a husband in his proper place. You, Claus, will do very nicely." And she returned to the bed and kissed him long and earnestly and went out the door.

THE GOLDFISH

And that was the way it happened. It was Marcy's ninth birthday and at the party little Hillary Nash came, all pigtails, glasses, and buck teeth and said, "Here's your birthday present, and where's the ice cream?" Everybody tittered politely and then Hillary said, "Oh, you better open them right now or they might die," and she ran into the next room laughing, and Marcy, green eyes aflame, eager hands flying over the ribbons and tissue, squealed "oh" with delight and her chubby fingers pulled out a gleaming fishbowl—and there were two goldfish, one the usual orange and gold and the other grey-black, looking more like a shadow than a fish.

Someone said, "Oh, a black goldfish!" And Marcy asked if there was a "gold blackfish," and the bowl was put on the mantle with the rest of the presents but not before Mother answered Marcy: "Oh, don't be silly! It's just like black sheep. Mamma Nature does it just for fun." But it wasn't until later when we tried to trace where the present came from did we find out much about the black one.

After the party, of course, Marcy went over her gifts one by one, carefully touching each one to see if she was dreaming, and then laying it aside for future reference: the games, the doll tea sets, and all. And then she came at last to the gleaming bowl. "This is my mostest favorite," she said. "I've never had anyone give me goldfishes on my birthday. And see! Here's the fish food and it says to feed them once a day."

And Marcy prattled on and on about the fish and Aunt Tomasina leaned over to tell Marcy not to put her hands in the water, that fish were meant to look at and not to play with and that she must keep them up high on the mantle because of Timmy the cat, and that was about all for that day except Gramps wandered in from outside where he had been hiding to keep away from the birthday party and the noise, and he said: "Gawd amight! Another pet, yet! We got cats, stray dogs, old mice, and now goldfish!"

But Marcy spoke up quickly defending her new pets: "But they don't make any noise, Grampy," she said, "and they don't eat much. See!" And Marcy held up her hands to show what a "tiny, tiny bit" the goldfish ate. But Gramps said, "Humph!" And he looked in the bowl and said humph again. "A black one, too! A mean little bugger if I ever saw one." And that was about all for that day. Except someone, I forget who, maybe Gramps said, "What you gonna name them?" And Marcy couldn't think and Gramps said, "To and Fro," and he laughed and slapped his good knee, but Marcy didn't think it was funny and she said, "No, my goldfish! I'll name them." And then she said "Goldy" for one and the black one she couldn't think of a name and Aunt Tomasina said, " 'Rumpelstiltskin,' maybe." And Marcy screamed, "No! No!"

"Not a bad name. The gold and then the bad dwarf with his black...." But then Gramps saw Marcy was beginning to cry. "Better we stick to To and Fro," he said and he went off to his room on the first floor and that was all about the goldfish for the first day.

On the second day Tomasina had to warn Marcy about the cat, Timmy; he had been looking up thoughtfully at the fish on the high mantle, and Tomasina said, too, not to feed them too much and to change their water once a week, but Gramps said, no, you don't change water much anymore because of the snails, and we all peered closely and sure enough there were two or three tiny snails and a long fern that coiled like a green snake about a sunken fish castle.

Nobody remembered seeing the castle before, or the white and blue pebbles on the bottom yesterday at the party, and Mother, who had strode into the room at this, spoke up in her loud voice and said she had gone down to the pet store—the only pet store in town—and she had gotten the pebbles and the castle with the hole in the middle, and that she had asked about the black goldfish and the man at the pet shop had said they were very rare, and that he had not seen any for a long time, and Mother, of course wondered then where the fish had come from because this would mean little Hillary's parents had driven over 60 miles to the city for the fish, and she said they would have to phone up the Nashes and thank them especially for such a nice, thoughtful present—and that was all about the fish on the second day.

On the third day, Gramps sat in his favorite chair, and he had put the fish bowl lower down on the record player near the window because he was going to be in the room and wanted to watch the fish at eye level, and Mother came in and warned him about putting newspaper under the bowl so as not to stain the dark walnut record player in case there was "any splashing" and Gramps was going to say that goldfish don't splash very much but he thought better of it for Mother was in one of her grumpy moods, and then Tomasina came in and reminded, "Watch out for Timmy, the cat."

"I'll bust him one with my cane if he comes near," Gramps said, and he then sat in the chair watching To and Fro, and the sunlight streamed through the bowl which acted as a prism and the light caught, too, on the shiny pearl and pinkish-colored pebbles on the bottom, and filtered through the rich, green, snake-like fern, and the two fish swimming—one gold as the summer sun, the other as a black shadow, seemingly not a fish at all, made a beautiful picture and Gramps was very content sitting in his chair just watching.

But after awhile, Gramps said to Aunt Tomasina, who had come back into the room, that To and Fro were not suitable names. "The gold one is *Fro* all right, but that black one—he sulks at the bottom and doesn't move much, except for some quick darts now and then, like an arrow. No, we'll have to call *him* something else." And Aunt Tomasina bent over the bowl and the black fish edged towards the surface and she could see his tiny eyes which were smoke-colored and like smoke seemed to move or float as stirred by a wind, and Tomasina suddenly straightened up and quickly went from the room and Gramps took his nap, then, sitting in the sunlight in his favorite chair, and lucky Timmy, the cat, was outside and couldn't get in for Gramps fell fast asleep.

But after awhile Gramps felt strange; it was like a shadow he said, later, that had come into the room, and he awoke from his nap with a start and he said he felt something was wrong and didn't know what it was. He was wide awake then and he saw the sun had fled the room, to be sure, and it looked like rain outside. But that wasn't it; Gramps felt uneasy in his bones.

And then his eyes fell on the fish bowl and the black one was no longer on the bottom next to the gaily-colored pearl pebbles, and in fact, Gramps couldn't see it at all at first, and then he saw a dark, slim shadow hiding in the long, snake-like fern, and then he saw the gold fish up above, highly agitated, swimming back and forth, and all of a sudden the dark fish darted up from the depths and took a nip at the gold one, and the gold one, swimming frantically, dodged around and around, and the dark one would glide like some tiny shark to the bottom, or like a submarine, Gramps said, and wait. And then when the gold one was still, it would come again.

Gramps watched this for quite awhile, and he thought the gold one would die of excitement and he called Tomasina and told her: "These here two fish are fighting and the black one's gonna kill the gold one, mark my word," and Tomasina, an old spinster and inclined to think about sex, said, "Bosh! It's some indecent mating dance or sex play which we know nothing about."

But Tomasina watched for awhile and the dark one attacked again and again, not with haste but with great slowness and deliberation, but persistent always, sliding up through the fern and coming in on the flank for a nip, and the gold one would be in a panic and whirl and twist and dodge at incredible speed, and Tomasina said again that it was some strange form of love play, and that was all for that day on the fish.

It was Marcy who saw them on the third day and she cried out in alarm at the sight of her beautiful gold one who seemed tattered and torn with bits of the fragile, delicate fins gone, and Gramps said that the black fish was always hungry and that he should be fed more and then wouldn't be so snappish. And Marcy quickly tore off a big chunk of fish flake food and crumbled it into the bowl and then she went off to school and Gramps shrugged his shoulders and went out for his morning constitutional, not that he needed the walk, but morning time was when Mother was most grumpy and it was best not to be around until after she'd had her breakfast and had tongue-lashed poor Tomasina a bit.

In the afternoon Gramps again took the gleaming bowl with the sunlight playing on the multicolored pebbles on the bottom and the black, black fish dormant next to the fern, and the restless gold one weaving to and fro, and put it on the record player with newspaper to guard the "splashing" where he could see the fish and the colors more easily, and held his cane at ready to ward off Timmy, the cat, lest he get any ideas, and he sat down in his favorite chair to watch, for somehow the colors glinting in the bowl were soothing to an old man, and he remembered the days when his own life had more color to it, and the days when Mother didn't nag so and his son-in-law was around and things had more order and shape.

And once again Gramps fell asleep and once again he woke up with a sudden start and he saw the black one's savage attack and he called aloud for Tomasina and even she was impressed this time. Tomasina said: "the black devil means to rape her, and I'll fix that!" And sure enough that very afternoon Tomasina marched herself to the pet shop and bought another bowl, for as she said the gold one looked "plumb peaked" dodging around, protecting her virtue, and she brought home a smallish bowl and a little cloth fish scoop and she and Gramps put the black one in the smaller bowl all by himself.

And Gramps moved the small bowl with the black fish in the kitchen, and when Marcy came home from school, Tomasina quickly said that the two fish had a lover's spat and they had taken up separate homes which was all right with Marcy for it was just like her mother and dad she said. "They're divorced! And my daddy's the black one!" And that was that for the day.

The next morning at breakfast, Gramps came down early for he always ate alone before the rest of the family was up for he thought we made too much noise, and he took the black fish and bowl down from a high window ledge, safe from Timmy, the cat, and put it down on the table while he ate his eggs and mush, and he said, "Now me black-hearted monster. Now, how do you like this?" And then as he watched, Gramps thought for a moment the black fish was dead for it had sunk to the bottom and lay motionless and nothing seemed to rouse it but Gramp's finger which he put in the water to see if he could stir it up some, and the fish came up then, a bit too quickly Gramps thought, its black snout pointing like an arrow, and Gramps pulled his finger out and said, "You're alive, you little black bastard! How do you like it alone, eh!"

And after breakfast Gramps went into the living room to see the gold one high on the mantle, and it seemed unholy restless, seeking in the green fern for its tormentor.

That afternoon at nap time, Gramps brought the black one in from the kitchen and placed the two bowls side by side, but

Tomasina said, "Oh, bosh! Fish can't see through those funny bowls at each other." But nevertheless Gramps said, "Oh, let them try peeking at each other." And so Gramps watched the sun pour into the bowls like liquid gold, and it made dazzling colors as it broke on the prism of the glass and sparkled on the colored pebbles and Gramps thought the colors soothing and after awhile Tomasina left the room to run errands for Mother and Gramps dozed off only to wake with a chill and his eyes searched quickly for the black fish for the sun had gone from the room, and the black one was highly agitated, whirling around and around in his small bowl as a dervish, turning end over end, and making other, strange, unfishlike movements. And Gramps thought he detected a small whirlpool made from the black one's quick movements and he was about to get more newspaper to protect the record player from splashing, but his eyes sought the other bowl and the gold one, too, seemed distressed and its movements were wild and nervous, just like the times when it had been quartered with her tormentor.

And Gramps thought well, maybe we were wrong—this was all mating play and they should be back together, and Gramps was about to change them and then he looked closely at the gold one with its naive, staring eyes, its saccharine, blank, insipid expression, and he said, "Well, now! I don't know about this!" And then he left the room and the two fish in their separate bowls were left on the record player for the night.

It was Tomasina who found the dead body of Timmy, the cat, on the living room floor the next morning and she emitted a high-pitched scream and everybody came running, and last came Gramps, but he didn't look at the cat on the floor but went straight to the fish bowls, and sure enough the gold one was gone, and Gramps couldn't see the black one anywhere—at least at first. But when Marcy said she saw the black one down at the bottom of the bowl, and she went to put her finger in to touch him to see if he was dead, and Gramps made a quick swat at Marcy's hand with his cane. "Gawd amight! Don't put your finger in there!" And sure enough, as Marcy withdrew her finger the black one moved swift as an arrow, but it was too late for him to nip Marcy's finger thanks to Gramps and his cane.

And Marcy began to cry then and Gramps said something about her being "a first born child," and Tomasina spoke up and

said, "That ain't no way for an honest goldfish to act," and that's
when Mother began to check on the present in earnest and she
called up the Nashes right away although it was only seven-
thirty in the morning and they liked to sleep fairly late, and they
acted surprised and said, no, they hadn't been to the city to get
any presents, not since Christmas time, and they'd ask little Hillary about the present and call us back.

And it turned out that "some man" had given little Hillary the
goldfish; a short man, little Hillary said, "something like Marcy's
daddy," but that was all anyone could get out of her. Mother then
asked to speak to little Hillary personally and she asked her a few
more questions over the phone, her voice getting loud and
scratchy, but then Hillary began to cry and Mother hung up
sharply, saying, "That damn little brat, she knows something!"
But we didn't dare ask Mother to explain and we all gave up on it
seeing as how Marcy knew that little Hillary was an "awful liar
sometimes," and I spoke up and said that Hillary could have
swiped the fish from the lake over at City Park and maybe spent
the money for Marcy's birthday present on candy, but then we
couldn't guess how she would get a fish bowl, and that anyhow
she didn't seem quite smart enough for all that trouble.

So, in the afternoon Gramps put some sort of lid over the small
bowl and we all went down to the pet shop and a short little man
there said he didn't quite know what kind of a fish the black one
was. "Some kind of tropic, perhaps," he said, and he seemed a
little embarrassed and the veins stood out in his neck and he
wiped his face with a handkerchief. And we all thought then the
pet shop man did look something like Marcy's dad, gone these
many years.

Gramps stood around for awhile in the store and Marcy ran up
and down looking at the turtles and the birds and all. But Gramps
kept coming back to the big fish tank, looking closely at the
goldfish, and as I was standing near him he said to me, "Funny,
they all remind me of someone I know very well. They have a
pop-eyed, self-aggrieved, long-suffering, prissy look in their
eyes I don't like..." And then he broke off, for Mother had come
up to him.

Pretty soon, Gramps, still standing by the fish tank, asked
the pet shop man would he take the black one to keep and the
little man said he would be glad to, and we all watched him as he

took a scoop and put the black one in the large tank with all the gold ones, and as soon as the black one hit the water the others— maybe thirty or forty of them—skittered away in endless golden ripples, wave upon golden wave, looking as they moved in flight like golden straw. And the black one sunk to the bottom of the tank glowering, and smoke seemed to curl up out of his tiny, tiny eye slits, and Gramps said, "A good nip now and then to let them know they're alive," to no one in particular. And that was all about the fish. Except on the way home Gramps leaned over to Tomasina and said, "You were right about the name."

"What do you mean?" answered Tomasina.

"Wanna make a bet Timmy died of eating spoiled... well, spoiled fish?" asked Gramps. But nobody answered him, and after awhile in the almost dead stillness of the car Gramps said, "Rumple, no Grumblestiltskin, and it serves him right!"

But finally, Aunt Tomasina said, "It's all about sex troubles of which we know nothing about," and Mother then spoke up in sort of a scratchy voice, "Hush! Tomasina, not in front of the children!" And we all rode back to the house in silence although Mother did begin to cry softly, staring blankly out the glass windows of the car.

AN EARLY FROST

I suppose, no, I'm certain it was not the want ad itself. It was the telephone number that caught my eye:

DEAD TREES RESTORED
If Your Favorite Tree Was Killed
By The Unseasonable Frost
Phone 777-7711

I fancy myself a good amateur gambler: cards, horses, fights, you name it. And I had asked the phone company years ago for just that number to go with my avocation or my personality, if you will. Phone company officials said that such an exchange was not possible in this area. Chicago yes, Centralia, no. In a fit of pique I called up the phone complaint department and made my pitch. No, one of those annoying voices said, after a ten-minute heel-cooling or ear-cooling delay, such a phone number could not be listed at Centralia. The newspaper ad made a mistake.

So, I called the number. Part of the attraction of the advertisement was that I was a chem and botany major in college; I knew no way of restoring dead trees myself, or I would have been up and at the task long before this. You see, I inherited this old place from my sainted Mother. Out in the backyard were her two favorite weeping willows where she used to sit reading Ronald Firbank and Jane Austen aloud to me in her shaky voice. Last September we had an early frost, killing the two willows plus an entire row of poplars that had served as a windbreak, and more practical service, to hide the garbage pail and trash bins. There were Mother's beautiful willows looking like so many sticks of bronze sculpture etched against the dark spring sky. Mind you, I'm not overly-sentimental or a tree lover especially, but the two willows were spaced just right for hammock hanging. My mother had raised them from a pup. So, what did I have to lose? Maybe fifty bucks to some phony nursery man who alleged he could save dead trees—trees stone dead more than seven months.

I dialed this number that the phone company said was non-existent. An answering service took my message. Two days later the phone rang, and a fairly pleasant voice said: "I'm Earl King!

I've come to save your trees!" There was an evangelical tone to the voice. We made an appointment for noon on the following day.

Noon, straight-up, there he was; he didn't ring the doorbell, but somehow I felt his presence. I'd just say he appeared in the vicinity of my front door, and I opened it. He was a twisted, gnarled sort; he reminded me of a timber-line spruce, bent by the wind. His skin had a funny yellow tinge to it, and his eyes, deep-set, were like floating marbles in an opaque, enameled sea. He had a little black doctor's satchel which he hugged close to his body.

All business-like, I conducted him to my twin willows. He knelt down and from the bag he took out a hypodermic syringe and filled it with some clear amber-colored fluid. The fluid looked to me somewhat like the old tincture of brownish soap we all used to shampoo our hair with. I recall I couldn't get close enough to smell the mixture, although I stood as close as I could when he stuck his needle near the base of the trees.

It, the operation, was all over in seconds. The syringe and amber fluid bottle were popped back into his satchel. "Fifty dollars down and fifty later, when your trees leaf out," he said.

I hesitated. "Ah... well," I stammered. "Somewhat reasonable, but how do I know this shot in my trees' fanny will work?"

"Good question," Earl King said "Give me a postdated check, three weeks from now."

"Got yourself a deal," I said. "Betcha another clean fifty, nothing happens."

"Not for a betting man," King said. "Hate to take sucker money. Candy from kids."

"Okay," I said. But I made the check out for four weeks ahead. Mr. King did not glance at the check but jammed it in his shirt pocket. "Be back someday soon," he said, and then he went quickly through my house and out to his car, a funny-looking foreign sedan. An odd car for a tree man, I thought as he sped away. No place to stow dead limbs and such.

In three weeks we were launched into our hot summer. The "we" is myself and my Mother's dog, Tooky, an old white Samoyed. Tooky often stretched out under the willows in the summer, and Mother would scratch his ears and they would both nap away the long afternoons. Much to my amazement, in the

stated time the willows leafed out. I hunted up the want ad then.
How dumb of me, I thought, not to have him give a shot to the
poplar trees while he was here. But then, alas, the bill would have
been more, and there might have been more risk with the poplars, which were dead as dead can be. I called 777-7711 anyway.
Nothing. Nothing, but a recording from the phone comany: "The
number you have dialed is not listed. Please ask information for
the correct...." I slammed the receiver down.

Well, to hell with it all, I thought. I called up my bank and
cancelled the check. Maybe that would bring Mr. King around.
The willows, meanwhile, blossomed out, greened out beauti-
fully. In fact, incredibly! Weeping willows have no blossoms, as
far as I know, and my trees were now covered with tiny red
blossoms, that gave off a rather strong, but delightful fragrance. I
was enchanted. I called back the bank to uncancel my check.
"What was the number of that check?" the teller asked. I looked
up my stub. "Ah...777," I said. "And then, 7711." Well, I had
made a mistake the teller said. My checking numbers were in the
zero, zero-twelve series. But anyway, no post-dated checks for
fifty dollars had been cashed on my account. So, I forgot about it
all.

I forgot about the trees, too, pretty much. I had to cut down a
good many branches to put up my hammock. The darn trees
were unusually lush. More like jungle growth than regular willow greenery. And there were strange-looking bugs flying
around underneath the two, and I spotted a green gecko lizard
zipping off into the grass, as I lay in my hammock. All in all, the
place didn't seem too pleasant a place to have a hammock anymore. But tradition is tradition. And I managed to lie there now
and then. It seemed uncommonly hot under all those sheltering
limbs now: humid, jungly. Not like a nice, orderly, weeping
willow in a town there 5,000 feet above sea level. But Tooky
seemed to like to stay out there.

And it was Tooky's strange death that made me start this
search. I found Tooky, who was old, it is true, and who did have
asthma, stone dead under the willows, his shaggy body covered
with yellowish pollen from these red flowers. To be sure, I took
Tooky to a vet and in my presence he began an autopsy. "Lungs
pretty good for an old dog," the vet said. "I dunno why he died.
Stroke maybe."

"Cut up the head," I said. "But I'll come back tomorrow." I couldn't stand to see old Tooky butchered this way.

"A complete autopsy will cost around one hundred," the vet said.

"Worth it," I said, and I wrote out a check and I almost put down the check number as 777-7711, but then I stopped myself.

Two days later the vet called. "I'm returning all but twenty dollars of your money. I don't know why the dog died. It just died. These things happen with older dogs."

"Well, I'm damned!" I said. And I went out then and lay down in the hammock with a novel by Firbank, *The Flower Beneath the Foot,* and a big glass of iced-coffee. This last so I wouldn't go to sleep. In twenty minutes or so there were all these tiny flowers drifting down on top of my hammock, and I was starting to be covered with a whitish, yellowish pollen, and I felt smothered: something like an asthma attack. And I got up in a hurry and took some of the pollen and a tiny blossom or two and put them under my own microscope, an instrument salvaged from my college days, and looked at these strange little spores and anthers. Never saw or heard of them in any botany text I had.

What to do? I'll get the son-of-a-bitch, I said. And I placed a want-ad in the local paper: "$500 reward for someone who can save my trees—killed by the Frost." No takers. Except a salesman from a nursery came out and tried to sell me an entire new landscape job.

So, I forgot about it all. Stayed out of my backyard entirely. Went to the horse races, played poker, came out way ahead, money-wise. Then I closed up the house, and moved to an apartment where I stayed until fall. The weather in Centralia then was unusually mild: Indian summer. But I did read in the papers how an "unseasonable frost" had killed all the trees in the small Colorado town of Big Junction. I said, *hmmm* to myself, and hopped in my car and drove some 400 miles to the town and holed up in a motel. Nothing much happened the first week; I mean, no interesting want ads in the local paper. So I drove to a larger town with a shopping center and bought a red wig, a false moustache, and heavy dark sun-glasses.

Then I came back to Big Junction and, under an assumed name, rented a large frame house that had a backyard full of frost-damaged trees, subscribed to the local paper, and sat back to

wait. I bought a white dog, too. This time a year-old Spitz.
About seven days later, there was the want-ad!

Call Earl King
If Your Trees Were
Damaged by Frost
777-7711

I called the number, gave my message to the answering service, and sat down at my front door to wait. Nothing happened. *Hmmm*, I said. I went to the local hardware store and bought a heavy spade and a 16-gauge shot-gun. And sat down again by my front door. Two days after this, about noon, I got a tingly feeling, and flung the door open. There he was.

"I'm Earl King, the tree man," he said. "Sorry, about the delay. Got tied up with some kids."

"How do you spell your first name," I asked. "E-r-l, or E-a-r-l?"

"Ah...ah...a misprint in the paper. But it's an old German name."

"From Konig?" I asked.

He gave me a hell of a penetrating look with those funny marble eyes. "How about your trees," he said in brisk, business-like tones.

"Trees? Right this way," I came back. I led him through the house to the backyard. My new white Spitz growled at him en route. "This weeping willow and those two poplars need fixing," I said.

When he bent down to open up his satchel, I struck him with the heavy spade that I had kept handy. Erl King, or whoever he was, slumped over without a sound. I was about to bash him another blow on the side of the head for good luck, but then I really had no evidence about Tooky's death. In fact, I wondered on just what impulse I had hit him at all. Perhaps I could take over his magic tree formula and make a bundle—but I didn't really need money that badly.

Poor man, I thought then. He never even tried to cash my fifty buck check. Well, what was done was done. Luckily, the house was isolated from neighbors and the backyard enclosed by a high fence; they'd find him next spring, if at all. I took his satchel, checking it first for the syringe and the amber fluid, jumped into my already-packed car and left town at a good clip. I drove to

Centralia, put the Spitz in a kennel, and then took a plane for Chicago and the small university where I got my biology degree.

Some two days later I was in the school lab with my old prof of bio-chemistry, Dr. Klein. My question was: "What is this stuff? It brings trees back to life." I added: "We can make a million!"

Working together, we ran the liquid through a detailed chemical analysis. This took the better part of a day, and at the end of that time, Dr. Klein threw up his hands. "I give up! You know this liquid looks and acts like snake-venom of some kind. And guess what?"

"What?"

"I've never seen the like before. An alkaloid base, some high density protein molecules, but... but...."

"Let's shoot some of the stuff in an old tree?"

"Well, maybe later," Dr. Klein said, "Right now let's shoot some in a white lab mouse."

Poor mousey was dead in thirty-nine seconds by a stop-watch.

"Well, now what?" Klein asked. "No dead trees around Chicago right now—that I know of."

"Get a two-day leave of absence from this jerk place and come out, at my expense, and look at my willow trees."

The three days I was in Chicago I, of course, bought all the Colorado newspapers I could lay my hands on. No mention of any dead or injured found in a yard in Big Junction. Luckily I had rented the old house there under a phony name. No way they could trace the real me; I mean, the Big Junction police would have a problem or two. I wasn't so sure about Mr. King.

En route back to Centralia, I told Dr. Klein the whole bit. Shortly after we arrived, I went to the boarding kennel to pick up my Spitz and left the professor snooping around my yard. He kept busy hacking away at the jungle-like branches and creepers, looking at the leaves and blossoms under my microscope. The damn trees meanwhile had usurped almost my entire backyard! Finally, we found the dead stumps of the old willows.

"This monstrosity you have here," Dr. Klein said then, "is a *new* tree, not a rebirth. This tree... ah... it's new to me. You sure your tree man didn't plant a few seeds while he was wielding the syringe?"

"What seeds could sprout into a tree in a few weeks?"

"Maybe he cast a spell, raised his arms in a benediction, whispered a magic incantation."

"Absurd! He bent down and stuck a needle in the trunks, and that's all."

"This monster here is something like the Banyan tree of India or maybe the peepul tree: all roots and creepers. If I don't miss my guess there's a snake skulking around its roots. Your dog, Booky? Tooky? It was bitten is my guess. A krait maybe?"

"Surely the vet could diagnose snake-bite?"

"Well, he'd know a rattler bite, being in Colorado. But a member of the *elapid* family—I don't know."

"Hah! An elaborate plan for some strange man to kill poor little me. Expensive, time-consuming, stupid! Why didn't he just shoot me?"

"He could have very well stabbed you with his needle. No noise. You'd be dead in two minutes. No one would know why or how."

"Or maybe I'd sprout into a Banyan tree? Absurd!"

"Ah...any bad gambling debts? I remember at college you were quite the one to...ah..."

"Nary a one! I'm clean as a whistle, welch-wise."

"What was the man's name again?"

"Earl King."

"*Das Erl Konig!* Ever hear of Schubert's song?"

"Oh, come on now, prof! Hear it? Why I can even sing it after a fashion. My mother's favorite."

At this, Dr. Klein looked at me sadly.

"All right!" I said with some irritation. "So, he's der Erl Konig. And he's 7,000 miles or more from his home base in Germany. And why me? Why me in this hunky mountain town in Colorado? And how do you figure I could bash him on the head with a shovel and not get hurt back, pronto?"

"Really doesn't add up very well," said Dr. Klein. "Just why did you hit him? We don't know why your dog Cooky or Hooky died."

"An impulse," I said. Klein sighed heavily at this. "Okay!" I said, "a *childish impulse*! But why does all this guff happen to me?"

"Job asked the same thing. Meanwhile, buy a mongoose; keep a shot-gun handy. Stay out of your backyard."

"Out of the yard!" I exploded. "Out of this damn town!"

"Well," Klein said then, "I wouldn't let any old Erlking push me around. He's supposed to annoy children, *only*, anyway. By the by, did you ever marry?"

"Well, up to now, I've been very comfortable here with my Mother and my...ah...habits," I answered. I was about to add, *you nosey old coot*, but I thought better of it.

I sent Dr. Klein back to Chicago the next day. What a sarcastic bastard, he was! I decided to put the old home up for sale, live in it until it was sold, and then clear out to New Zealand or some far off place. No sense letting a German mythological character get the best of me. I didn't get a mongoose, of course, but I kept my 16-gauge shotgun handy. And I put out a pan of milk; poisoned, of course, and I kept my doggy inside.

Really, I didn't want to stay in the old house, but it was more convenient to do so; potential buyers dropped in at all hours, and it was best that I be on hand instead of some indifferent real-estate agent. So I stayed on. One time, early in the morning, I woke up with a strange tingling sensation. I ran to the bedroom window that looked out on the backyard. In the dim light, I swear, I saw my mother resting in the hammock, scratching old Tooky's ears. I tried to call out to her, but I seemed paralyzed.

After that, I thought I would lose my mind. So I started to drink heavily. I had plenty of time, too, to reflect about Mother, about my past. About Dr. Klein's question, damn him; *why didn't I ever marry?* Why the hell didn't I? Too comfortable being a bachelor. Don't get me wrong; I had girl friends. But they meant trouble, responsibility. I got rid of them fairly quickly. None of them ever matched Mother for understanding, for good cooking, for...for sympathy. So I didn't grow up exactly; I mean, mature. But really nobody's damn business. Mother left me considerable money, and so...And so?

But the Erlking comes for all children—if they remain children too long, that is. I read up on the old German folk-tale. This evil spirit was meant to frighten *kinder* when they'd been bad. But he supposedly carried off quite a few also...to...to Erl King land, I guess. I read about the Banyan tree, also. *Ficus Bengalensis*. Sometimes the tree would grow and grow and whole villages could settle under the branches. But there were disturbing folk tales about dark spirits inhabiting the Banyan; one could easily imagine the snake-like roots reaching out at night to crush a victim. Truly, not a pleasant tree to have in one's backyard; I think it hurt the sale of the house, too. Potential buyers would be pleased about the house until I conducted them to the yard, and then there would be silence and a hasty departure.

But I kept to my post. Perhaps there would be an early frost and it would kill every damn thing in the yard: snakes, roots, lizards, Lord knows what. But then this thing about my dreams. The dreams, at least, defeated me. I'm not a coward exactly. I didn't quite dare lie out on the hammock underneath the willows, but on a garden lounge chair fairly nearby.

I decided the last night, my last night, in the real world, to sleep out in the yard all night. I had my shotgun and a quart of gin. Mother drank gin; tradition is tradition. I drank myself into a stupor, and fell asleep. I dreamt that a very large cobra was twining about the willow trees, the Banyan tree. And then, in this last dream of mine I felt—no, I knew! I knew that I was the tree, a young tree, a child of a tree. I kept calling for my mother, and then . . . and then . . . the cobra spread its hood, an enormous hood that blotted out the sky, and struck out at me. I remember I got up from the lounge chair screaming. "Quick! Mother! An antidote!"

But there was no one there. Nothing. I wrote Dr. Klein right after the nightmare. A rambling incoherent letter. Something about the Earl King. I got one back, almost immediately:

> Dear Tooky: I'm more disturbed about you than any shrubbery in your backyard. Due to smog, etc., the polar caps are melting and our climate is changing. Tropical plants will be common in your area. But you, Phocian, why don't you get married and settle down? Quit brooding about your Mother and the past. The Banyan tree is in your mind, *ncest pas?* Just for kicks, see a headshrinker?

Horse manure to you, old buddy, I thought. But then, Dr. Klein with his twisted frame, and funny eyes—eyes twisted from peering into microscopes, reminded me of Earl King. I sent him an air mail letter right back which said: "I hate you, Earl King Klein."

So? So, I took his advice and went into group therapy. Damn, if somehow, Dr. Klein, in a sense, had me committed. The doctor and the rest, they laugh at me. But I know there was an Erl King, and he'll come for me someday. Although I do feel somewhat safer here in the rest home with the drugs and all. But he'll come for me—I know it, I know it! Just the other day there was an early frost.

If only Tooky were here to bite someone for me. If only my mother . . . she . . .

THE FERRARI

One time, last summer to be exact, I was just about to kick my little foreign car in its tail pipe and walk to work the rest of my life, when I decided to give the thing one more chance.

The car was one of those little spinebreakers with motorcycle springs, a low center of gravity, and an odd-ball cooling system. This last meant vapor locks for the gas line and ulcers for me; in fact, when it sputtered out in downtown traffic, I was just about fed up.

"Social life," I said to myself as I aimed a kick at the car. "Your social life seems to pick up with a foreign make." "Well, okay," I said to myself, "I'll get this fixed one more time. But the social life better be damn good."

So I stopped talking to myself and began to look around for a repair shop. And this all led, in a roundabout way, to my having a fairly interesting summer—a summer involving an $18,000 racing car, a stinker, a damsel with grease stains on her leg, and Lord knows what all.

Via the foreign-car driver's grapevine, I heard about a mechanic who had a good grease-rack manner; i.e., he didn't mind using metric tools, and more important, he would put up with the customer's mother-hen attitude. The garage was way out in the suburbs—a good sign, for cheap garage rent might mean lower repair bills. The garage itself was not as down-at-the-heel as I had hoped. It served both as an agency for a number of the major sports cars and as a repair shop. A sign in the window said the owner and chief mechanic was Frank Gighlardi who, the sign went on to say, once drove in the Memorial Day race at Indianapolis.

The showroom floor had several brand-new models and a few of the old classic cars. As I recall, there was a blue-trim Porsche, a Lancia Spyder, a Lister Maserati, a 1930 Mercedes-Benz, and off to one side, an old, brass-plated Lagonda, the kind of a car movie stars used to buy in the 1930's. In the repair shop were two cars of racing caliber. One was a stripped-down Jaguar, and the other a long, red and cream-trim auto I didn't recognize.

I quickly looked around the shop for one of the small, egg-beater, gas-saver types, because a garage full of high priced cars was a bad sign. I said hello loudly several times and walked towards the rear. Just then I heard the roar of a motor, the high-pitched, flutey roar that means twelve cylinders, dual exhausts, and superchargers. Someone was gunning the long red and cream car, and as I came near I saw it was a magnificent Farina Ferrari: the kind that sends the sport car fan into a state of shock. In a moment, a mechanic, dressed incongruously in street clothes and a pearl gray fedora, pulled back from the hood of the Ferrari and said, "Hi! Boy, doesn't she sound like . . . like a fine gold watch?"

"Just like the hum of a twenty-jewel top," I said entering into the game. Lord knows why foreign car owners don't gag to death on the corny comments about the sounds of their motors.

"Just like the clink of 18,000 golden dollars on the counter," the mechanic said.

"Just like the hum of a fan dancer's behind," I came back. And then we both laughed.

"I'm Frank Gighlardi," the man said. "Maybe you heard of me. I drove in the big race."

"Sure thing," I said. Then I said quickly, "I'm here about my little car," in hopes he wouldn't start a long flashback on his racing career.

"Be with you in a minute," Frank said, and he went back to the Ferrari, and as he carefully lowered the hood, I had a glimpse of chrome plated pipes, and two giant carburetors; it was almost like looking into a show window at Tiffany's.

"Is that what this baby cost—18,000?" I went around front and kicked at the tires mounted on trim wire racing wheels.

"That's with no extras. No extras atall."

"With all these high priced cars around I guess you don't work much on these little wagons?" I asked.

Frank squinted a pair of pebble-brown eyes at me and ran his large, grease-stained hands along the sleek, cream fender of the Ferrari. "You got me wrong. A lot of my customers aren't in the chips. Why, would you believe it, this Ferrari here I'm just about to sell it to a kid and his wife. I don't think they make a hundred a week between 'em. And both of them working night and day. God knows how they're going to make the payments—a hundred dollars a week." Frank laughed, a heavy, guttural laugh. "They've saved up—I mean they've almost saved up enough to make me a down payment."

"You're kidding," I said. "Ferraris aren't for working folks."

"No," Frank said. "They mean it. They're living in a cold water flat. No heat, no nothing, I guess. All their money, and I mean *all* of it, is gonna go on payments for this thing. Just car-happy that's all."

"It's a religion," I said.

"Yeah. That's good! A religion."

That was all the conversation I had with Frank that day. He looked over my little car, grunted a price, and I left it with him. I couldn't get the young couple out of my mind, though. Nobody, I thought, in this day and age, had that much economic guts.

A week later Frank phoned and said my English eggbeater was partly ready. He had had some trouble getting parts, naturally, and it wasn't exactly fixed, but he wanted to get the car out of the way. All he'd managed to do was wrap the gas line with asbestos, and he said that that would relieve the vapor lock until he could get me an electric fuel pump attachment. So you see what I mean about getting foreign cars fixed. When they go haywire you mostly ride the trolley bus.

I picked up the car the same day, and I saw the long Ferrari was out of the shop. As I paid my preliminary bill, I mentioned the big car. "I see the kids managed to scrape up the down payment on the diamond-studded sports job," I said.

"Yep," Frank said. "The poor suckers. I delivered it yesterday. They gave me $3,000 cash. God knows how they got that kind of money. They must have hocked everything they owned in the world. Well, they'll never see that dough again, anyway. Only about $15,000 more for them to go!"

"They could have bought a new house," I said.

Frank laughed at this. "My customers don't care much about houses. The poor jerks will never make it—never! You should have seen the shack they was living in. No self-respecting ground hog would hole up there. What some people won't do for a fast car."

"A religion," I said, and Frank smiled a twisted sort of smile. "Yeh, you're right. A religion."

I drove away, bouncing in my car towards town. The garage and Frank had suddenly put me in the dumps. It was his manner when he talked about the kids, I guess. Imagine the nerve! It was easy to piece together, and driving home that day I amused myself by filling in the large gaps missing from Frank's cryptic information.

I decided to call the story "My $18,000 Romance." The boy was a slim, blond, Nordic type, I decided, and the girl was rather plain with a snub nose, but she had striking Irish-blue eyes, a lithe, supple figure, and breath-taking creamy white skin—a skin something like the color of the fenders on the Ferrari. They'd met at a sports car club, of course. The boy had a second-hand MG that he'd traded for his mouse-grey Chevvie. He talked nothing but dual exhausts, jet carbs, and torque thrust. The girl could parrot the jargon, too, after a fashion, so they got on pretty well from the start. She had no car herself, but came to the first meeting of the sports club with a senile playboy in an old Cord.

She had drifted toward the boy from the start, and soon they were dating fairly steady. They'd go for a breezy, windy ride in the little MG, and their talk would be sprinkled with such terms as nave plates, fascia, and drop heads, and they'd look long and lovingly at the R.S. cars the other and wealthier members had. One day they had ended up at Frank's shop for minor repair work on the MG. There had been the sleek red Ferrari, sitting in the show window—a symbol of all their dreams.

Finally, the dream ran away with both of them; that's all. The girl was the catalyst. She was out to get the boy, and competition was keen. A widow in the sports club had an Austin-Healey and was on the make for any young male flesh. The girl had seen the gleam in the boy's eyes when they had examined the Ferrari, and she hoped such a gleam would some day shine for her. But the way to that boy's heart was not through sex or the stomach, but, of course, through the Ferrari.

Slowly, carefully, she built the dream for him. "If we were both working," she said, "maybe we could swing it. My folks might give me a wed... well, a present, if..."

The boy had picked up the cue readily enough. They were married: a quickie affair, driving across the state line to a justice of the peace with a few of the sport club fans along. The widow had joined the wedding party, too, and she had led all the way in her Austin-Healey, throwing back dust on the open MG.

On their brief honeymoon, the kids went back to look at the Ferrari in the show window. The girl had not been lying exactly about a wedding dowry. Her folks were strictly middle-class and could see a silver tea set and maybe a cedar chest, but no cash on the line. But they did have a small bungalow used as rental income, and this property was turned over to them with the expectations they would make this their first home. Of course, the two got a mortgage on the bungalow the next day to help make the down payment on the Ferrari.

The girl kept her job—she was a typist for some oil firm downtown. The boy had a job selling classified ad space for the local paper. And actually, that's how he had gotten to know Frank a bit better, trying to sell him space for an ad on the Ferrari. Then the kid had gotten a job nights in a bakery, which meant, all told, working from about nine a.m. until three a.m. six times a week. The girl, too, took on extra typing jobs at home, and so maybe their income was up to some $125.00 per week.

Meanwhile, the Ferrari wasn't selling; it sat in the showroom, mainly, for hardly anyone in the area would be so rash as to invest that much for transportation or status seeking. Frank really never expected the car to sell, even though he bought quite a few ads from the kid. Frank saw the car as a publicity device—to attract sport car fans to his showroom. Then, too, he planned to enter the car in a race, again for publicity reasons, and thus find money from a sponsor.

But finally, the kids sold Frank on their dream—or so they thought. And Frank's brown pig eyes gleamed along with theirs. He'd get a large down payment, and then in a few months, more than likely, get the car back as good as new, sell it second-hand for a thousand or so less and be far ahead.

Well, through the car, and her folks' rental property, the girl had gotten the boy. There had been no other way. When she saw this gleam in the boy's eyes she tried to tell herself it was a Nordic fire for adventure. Maybe her boy had old Viking blood and the car would give him a ship to conquer the world. No, more than that. The car would give him wings. It would be his sword, too,

and his Viking cudgel; his charging red steed of knighthood.
And then she would be in the dream, too, forever. Her Austin-
Healey rival would be lost in the flamboyant dust. She would sit
by his side, slipping through the night at a speed unknown to
lesser men. They would pass every car on the road. They would
escape, and outrun life itself—death itself. Nothing could touch
them in the red, magic car. Nothing could catch them.

A month or so later Frank called me about the part on my car.
Or rather, I called Frank. Yes, the part had come in. He'd been too
busy to phone. His voice gave me a chill. What he had meant by
not phoning was that there wasn't much profit in fooling with my
eggbeater, and so why bother. Besides, Frank's tone of voice
implied that his was the only decent foreign car shop in town. I
should grovel and beg a little. As I hung up, I could see right then
my kids wouldn't have a chance.

The first thing I saw in the garage was the red Ferrari—long
and shining as the sword of Siegfried. Frank was there, wearing
his pearl gray fedora and business suit, giving the car a tune-up. I
asked him casually, in between motor roars, about my two brave
kids, and Frank laughed his strange guttural laugh.

"Ha! I got the kid over a barrel already," he said. Why Frank, at
this point, took me into his confidence, I don't know. Except that
the people who drive the little gas-saver cars are usually mice
who don't count much and can't do anything about justice or
injustice, anyway. "A tune-up job on this thing costs a good
two-hundred smackers, but I'm giving it to the kids free. Part of
the service, I told them."

Frank revved the motor up to 8,200 and the shop walls seemed
to tremble. "Lissen to that baby purr," he said. "Like a...like
a..."

"Like the sound of 10,000 hornets," I said.

"Good!" Frank said. "I'll remember that one. But no! It's more
like...like the sound of the wind...like...like..."

"Like a hurricane sweeping up the coast."

"Smooth as a baby's behind," Frank said. "And I'm thinking of
a certain baby I know."

I waited around while Frank expertly hooked up my new fuel
pump to the gas line. I watched his big, grease-smeared hands
wrap around my little car's motor as he worked. My car must be

choking, I felt. When he was finished, I paid the bill and then I stalled around. I was hoping Frank would talk about the kids. As casually as I could, I asked: "How... how the kids coming? They keeping up on the payments?"

Frank laughed and his eyes looked straight into mine. The eyes seemed a jet black in the dim light of the shop. "Not that I care," I said hastily. "I was just wondering."

"Ha! Lemme tell you! Lemme tell you! You wouldn't believe it. This car ain't here for a tune-up, exactly. The kid got a speeding ticket. He's been kicked off the roads until they scrape up the fine—forty-five bucks. This is the second time he's been tagged. He made the mistake of trying to run away. Dammit! The car will run away from anything the police have got—anything in three states. But of course, not the telephone. The cops were laying for him back at his home."

I sensed right away the patrol had called Frank, asking for the home address of the Ferrari owner, and Frank had obliged.

"First time," Frank went on, "the speeding fine is ten. They had paid that somehow. Probably didn't eat that week. But the second fine was $45.00, and the cops know them sport car drivers can't help letting her out. All the roads around here are restricted at 60 for top speed. A Ferrari is just loafing in second gear around that. Well, now they got to make their weekly payments, plus the forty-five before he can drive it again."

"Well, how come..."

"I'm getting to that. They put it in the police garage, but I bailed it out. Now they have to pay me. But not in money." Frank laughed a high-pitched laugh this time. "Not in money..."

That's all Frank told me then. A customer had come in with a Singer that was wheezing out of tune, and he left abruptly and went over to the ailing car. I didn't have to wonder what Frank had meant by saying, not in money. I could see it all in my mind and I wrote the second chapter of my $18,000 Romance as I jarred home in my little car.

Frank had agreed to let one weekly payment go by. The couple had come in to get the car. Frank said he had tossed in a free tune-up job—that he was on their side, all the way. The kids were deliriously happy and thought Frank was a prince. Just before they were to leave in the Ferrari, Frank got the girl alone in his back office and had made a pass—a very definite pass. He'd stated the proposition to her directly, hemming her in behind his desk and a chair. She was to come back some night soon while the kid was working at the bakery and make her payment. The girl broke away then, but not before Frank had let her know he meant business.

"Okay! Okay!" she had whispered and had run out to the red Ferrari waiting at the curb, its beautiful motor humming like the sound of a high wind on a winter night. Frank had known that if the boy lost the car, the girl would lose the boy.

Late that night, as they both undressed for bed, the boy had spotted grease marks on the girl's leg; the black smear showed up clearly on the creamy white skin.

"Honey," the boy had said, "you look like you almost got a grease job."

"Oh," the girl stammered. "I...I...went to the restroom at the garage. While you were warming up the car. Dirty in there," she said. "Dirty."

The boy had laughed then, but the girl quickly snapped off the lights and began to cry. The girl cried most of the night, too. When the boy was asleep she had gotten up to wipe the grease stain off her leg with cold cream, but she could still see a faint smudge. She realized then that the Ferrari really hadn't rescued them from life; life was faster than the machine, after all. And death was faster, too. She just couldn't go through with it with Frank. She had to get money another way.

In the morning the girl sat on the side of the bed, combing her long dark hair and looking down at the boy. "Darling," she had said. "I...I...don't like favors from Frank. We've got to pay that fine money somehow. We've just got to!"

The boy didn't argue. He reached for her suddenly, pulling her to him. In a minute he pushed her away. "Jesus," he had said. "I'm too tired lately. Too tired for anything. My jobs, the car. My jobs, the car."

"Money," the girl said. "We've got to pay Frank the money."

"Yeh. I guess you're right," the boy said. "No sense losing a friend."

The next day both of them went to the hospital on their lunch hours and sold blood at $25.00 a pint. The girl watched as her blood ran into a jar. "Funny," she had told the boy later, "if we scratch the paint on our car, we can use blood to touch it up."

They had paid Frank back his fine money then. Frank had accepted the money in good grace, so the girl thought. Like all racing men, he had learned to be a good loser. They had both gone to pay Frank the money, and as he walked back to the car he had put a grease-stained hand on a long, creamy fender. "Well, no more drag races, kid," he had said. "I can't bail you out next time. The fine jumps to something like two-hundred bucks if they catch you again." Frank had touched the fender again, stroking it and smearing grease along the paint, and a frown passed over the boy's face. The girl then had reached out quickly and had wiped the fender clean with her handkerchief.

"Oops! Sorry," Frank said. "Glad to see you take good care of your... fenders." They had started to drive off then, but Frank spoke out: "Watch out now, too, for them dumb Sunday drivers around. A new fender costs about $800 on these babies. Yah gotta take the whole side off—maybe send to Italy for door clamps and stuff. You watch out, now!"

The kid had smiled wanly at this and they had driven off, the motor humming ominously like the voice of a prophet in evil times.

This parting shot of Frank's about Sunday drivers had done the trick, though. The kids were now almost scared to take it out in traffic, and Sunday was the only day they had time to drive it. High speed on the highways was at an end, too. The police had them tagged and filed. They just might as well have had a German Gesundheit gas-saver.

I had no occasion to visit Frank's garage again for a long time—maybe three months. The new fuel pump worked well enough and hadn't needed any adjustment. My little car hummed along, sounding like... well, not like a fine watch, but like a pretty good dollar one: click, cluck, click.

But then one day I thought maybe I'd have someone fix my turn indicator; they were always going haywire on the English cars, and it meant I had to open the window and stick my cold hand out in the wind, hoping to God some truck driver would see it wagging in the night. I tried the one other foreign repair shop in town, because I really didn't care to have anything more to do with Frank and his ways, but the other shop, of course, didn't have the parts and the mechanic there was rather vague about the length of time I'd have to wait, so I drove on out to Frank's.

I had a bunny-hop feeling in my stomach as I clicked-clucked into the garage, but the red Ferrari wasn't there. Maybe the kids had beat the game after all. Frank was rather glum and noncommital. Yes, he'd fix the turn indicator, but he'd have to wire Chicago for a part and it would take two weeks. As I left—I couldn't help myself—I asked: "How are the kids coming?" Frank stared at me blankly. "I mean the Ferrari twins."

"Oh, them Ferrari twins! That's a good one! I'll have to remember that crack. Gawd, there's nothing like a kid that's foreign-car-happy. You know they're keeping up on the payments! I went to get the money the other day when they were late. There was the car sitting out in a shed back of their rat hole. It just sits there all day now. They can't afford to drive it." Frank laughed and his eyes seemed to turn a grey-greenish color. "Tell you the truth. They can't afford an oil change. Would you believe it! The Ferrari takes 14 quarts of oil at a crack. It's gotta be good clean oil all the time in that motor. So it just sits there. The kid polishes it all the time, and it shines like a . . . like a . . ."

"Like a red gold piece on a silver mirror," I said, shooting from my verbal hip.

"Good," Frank said. "That's a good one. On Sundays they polish it. Polish it all day long. I told him you take better care of your car than you do your teeth. But the kid didn't laugh and the girl said that he had paid more for the car than his teeth. Sometimes they sit in the car all day. And all night, too, I think because they're afraid of teen-age vandals or car strippers."

"Nice place to sit," I said. "An $18,000 throne."

"But I got an ace in the hole," Frank went on. "The girl's gonna have a baby now. I seed her all swelled out like a . . . like a . . ." Frank looked at me for the expected aid.

"Like a heat blister on a second-hand tire," I said. It was the best I could do.

In three weeks my turn indicator part had come in and Frank phoned me. Business was dull, I guess, and so he had time to pay attention to his pin-money customers. I came chugging in in my little jewel-box and there, of course, was the Ferrari sitting in the show window looking aloof, inviolate and untouched as some Greek goddess. It had a big placard across the windshield. "Sacrifice," the sign said.

I didn't talk to Frank that time. One of his white-coated assistants installed the part as I waited. I saw a glimpse of Frank once in the back office as I paid my bill. It seemed to me, in the brief glance, that Frank was sporting a large purple and greenish-looking black eye. But then maybe not.

I really didn't need to quiz Frank to get the rest of the story. The girl had done this. The only way to win her boy back to life was to have a baby. She had to stop work and he couldn't possibly make it alone. They had to get rid of the Ferrari. The baby was on the way, and of course the boy had fussed and fumed. They were losing their $3,000 down payment. He was losing his reason for being alive—or so he thought. The old Nordic, Faustian fire had gone out of his eyes for good then, I guess. But the girl didn't really care. She knew the fire had died down long before that. It died on one dull Sunday when they had spent the whole day just sitting in the car while the kid had polished the chrome dashboard, and the impressive, sparkling dials. They had had nothing to eat that whole day but cornflakes and water. The only decent thing they had had to eat all week was one hot dog apiece at a sidewalk stand. A week before that they had one good meal at the girl's folks—and the kid hated going there for meals because mother-in-law nagged about the car and the payments, and the mortgage on the bungalow.

I don't know what to say about the last chapter of my $18,000 Romance. When a kid's car-happy there's no passion quite like it. The machine, or the speed of a machine, is some 20th century disease, that's all, related to the ailment Icarus had when he flew on wax wings toward the sun. The boy lost the Ferrari and maybe he thought it was all the girl's fault. For having the baby, I mean. Then there was that wealthy widow with the Austin-Healey and a yen for young boys. So, I don't really know about that last chapter.

Sometimes in a waking-dream I see the three of them driving along the highway in an old, Chevvie four-door. The kid would always have to have some kind of steed. Maybe he was just a Sancho Panza on a donkey now, but riding, anyway. The girl, with the baby in her arms, is smiling at the boy as they chug along. A chopped-down hot rod has just passed them—the kind of an R.S. that wouldn't come within eighty miles of a Ferrari on a foggy day.

The girl sees a twinge across the face of the boy, and a spark of the old Nordic fire burns in his eyes. Then the boy yells suddenly at the hot-rodder: "Go ahead and pass me! You can all pass me!"

But the girl knows he doesn't mean it. Maybe she senses that having a wife and family isn't enough for the 20th century man. He wants speed and the stars, and the wife and kids are minor episodes. Well, maybe after a while the girl went back to her folks, and pretty soon along came a man in a little gas-saver car—a man who'd bet on flesh and blood over oil and cylinders. A man who knew a good thing when he saw it. I mean heard it.

THE RHYME IN FREDDY'S FACE

We didn't come often, Sikes and I, for we had nothing to say. But then, Freddy had not much to say to us. But at that time I had two television sets, and I brought Freddy one of mine for he had been renting one; no sense buying anything when you have cancer of the face, and so I had an excuse to come up to see how the set was acting. Did it need a new tube? No, Freddy said. It was fine, but only one of his eyes, by that time was working. "I don't watch it too much. But it's about all I have." This last so as not to make me feel like a Lady Bountiful, an ass.

But this was not quite true. Freddy had a sister in Chicago, and once in awhile the two lesbians in our department would come and take Freddy out for an airing. But I think the sister should have done more. And then again, she was married with two kids, troubles of her own. What the hell could she do, come out and hold his hand to the unpleasant end? I said, go to Chicago, they have better doctors there. What I meant was: please have the kindness not to die in front of our eyes. Freddy said, no, Denver was good enough. He'd "feel terrible" around his sister. They were never too close.

She did finally come out when Freddy died. I got my portable TV set back, just barely, as the sister cleaned out his small apartment. But there really was nothing to clean out—just empty whisky bottles, and gin bottles and vodka bottles, and half-filled bottles of pain and sleeping pills, and a few dusty manuscripts of what were once things on the way to be poems, I suppose. God help us all.

I was sent to teach his class once, near the end. We were both underpaid English teachers in a small private college. He had, incredibly, signed up for work with his face half gone, and his mouth and lips split in two, and half of his freshman comp students had walked out. But bravely, insanely, he taught two sections of comp—or tried to. The college was too small to have any decent sick-pay plan. I have tried in my mind to visualize him in front of that wiggly, bored comp class, attempting to articulate words, trying to say something intelligible about the semicolon through the bandages, and each day getting weaker, his voice fading, sitting at the desk in front of them with his head in his hands, uncorrected theme papers heaped on his desk, a few sensitive girls sitting in the front rows crying, a few boys in the back seats, happily asleep, planning to go to the office the next day and ask for a tuition refund, God knows what.

Why would he do all this? This grim, Puritan ethic that taught him to be faithful to the last breath, to the last piece of chalk and the last sentence fragment. He was hardly Browning's *Grammarian*, seeking knowledge, seeking some integrity. He, in truth, was an unfortunate homosexual, tricked by an angry God. But the gods know he was brave. Brave and senseless at the same time, like life.

It's not that I, for one, hadn't seen death before, or death's aftermath, or if you like, its beforehand. I was in an army hospital after the war, and there were the paraplegics, wired to their beds forever with an umbilical cord attachment from their dead bladders to a plastic pot, and after awhile they would give up and die. And in the war we'd use flame throwers, and actually deep-fry a man like you would a doughnut. And let's say I was pretty numb about things like that: either slow or fast deaths.

I mean, you get numb in this life or you crack up completely, that's all. But this calling on Freddy was different. Sikes and I, sweaty in our tennis clothes, bounding up the rickety stairs to see him, and there, opening the door to our knock, would be Freddy with his terminal face cancer. And what the hell could we say or do?

I imagine, we looked to him the picture of health, two fresh boys full of vim and vigor, bursting with energy, and there was the fact of Freddy before us; nine-tenths dead, I suppose. But still a straw dummy, a facsimile of a man; except for a huge bandage on his right cheek and his split lip, in fair good shape; still alive, and able in a lisping fashion to talk to us, and drink with us, and tell us of his plans to put out a book of poems, "my last poems," although, really, he hadn't any first poems. Just last ones.

Why Sikes and I ever came to see him, we didn't quite know. The TV set was too threadbare an excuse. Perhaps some vague sense of duty; we were not too close, but he was a colleague of ours in the English department and we were nudged very slightly by John Donne's sermon, of course. And as I said, when the docs split his mouth to get, surgically, at the face cancer, a cancer edging ever nearer to the brain, he finally had to drop out of teaching, for mainly, towards the last, the kids couldn't understand him. And we could only pretend to while he lisped drunkenly about his poems. And we made small talk, ghastly chit chat, "Can we bring you anything?" A noise that sounded like no. "Go for a ride in the mountains?" No answer to this last. Freddy merely smiled into his vodka glass, and we sat there numb.

Afterwards, Sikes and I went to get a boiler-maker. A stiff drink should have, but did not, wipe it out. Wipe the picture out. I mean this picture, this infernal snap shot, I now have in my mind forever. Like Keats and his Grecian urn. Sikes and I standing there, drenched in sweat in this tiny flat, our semi-white tennis shorts, our rackets. There we are frozen in time, facing Freddy with his face half gone, mumbling hello, we brought some beer, thought you'd like to talk.

Sometime, during the painful twenty minutes or so we were there, I had walked into the kitchen to get ice for his drink and there were whisky and gin bottles and coke bottles and mixer bottles from one end of the kitchen to the other. What else was there to do but drink and drink some more? And I wanted to search in his medicine cabinet for the pills, the pain pills, the sleeping ones, wherewith I'm sure he could have put himself out of it at anytime, but didn't for some unaccountable reason. Maybe to shame Sikes and myself for our health, and good luck, to teach us some obvious lesson that life and health and luck on the tennis courts are only transitory things, and that you, too, can have face cancer and crumble away, piece by piece in front of your friends.

What torture this dying of cancer—something like Houseman said to rhyme your friends to death before their time sort of thing. I mean, the rhyme was in Freddy's face for all of us to read. And maybe here was some bittersweet victory in this for him, I don't know. But he hung on. And hung on like someone addicted to the Puritan ethic that suicide was bad, that it is our bounded duty to drink these drinks we have to the dregs; I don't know.

But it couldn't have been this really, for Freddy was hardly the last Puritan. As I said, he was a homosexual, but the unobnoxious, unobtrusive kind. I first met him in grad school, and he had,

I guess, a mild crush on his writing instructor, and would talk to him privately of jack rags, and other paraphernalia the homos used, or their jargon at least. And I was rather repelled at the time. Freddy, then, had been a tall, almost excessively handsome youth, with chestnut brown hair, perhaps curled or marcelled, but very likely, natural. He had pleasant, non-descript eyes, hazel perhaps. I never would have noticed him if our writing instructor, a curt, blunt little man, name of Owens, hadn't cornered me one time in a bar, and we talked of Freddy, or rather, Owens mentioned his disgust over how the writing trade attracted homos. He said, too, Freddy carried a tube of vaseline with him—just in case. So I, for one, pretty much avoided Freddy at school. My own life was troubled enough without getting a pass from a homo, and even a slight gesture of friendship on my part, might bring embarrassment. He got his sex, I heard later, by picking up young boys in restrooms. He was beaten up something awful once (about the face) by a gang of toughs on a "pansy-knocking" party. And who knows, this beating might have spawned the face cancer, but I prefer now to think it was merely the whimsical prank of the gods.

But anyway, there was something that repelled you about Freddy, even without prior knowledge of his sexual tastes; or perhaps it was his aloofness. He didn't want you to suspect he was a homo, and the only way for him was isolation and withdrawal, I suppose. And this was why, I guess, he was mostly alone in his little flat. Not even a bathroom. In the mornings he would have to trudge down the long hallway, his face buried in bandages, and use a common W.C., and he must have felt the shudders and disgust of other roomers, who felt that he might contaminate them somehow.

But in marriage, ordinarily, he would have had a wife to make these last few weeks bearable. Perhaps a wife does this, but I don't know for sure. But the emptiness of his rooms struck us like a blow in the face. There was no one there but Freddy and his empty gin bottles, his bandages, and once in a great while us, bounding up the stairs that last hot summer of his life... to...to...what? Stare at his bandage, pretend with him that his poems would be published. To talk of what?

I wanted to explain, for one thing, that I wasn't so damn healthy. That I had asthma, that I played tennis at great risk to the breath of life. That Sikes, too, had troubles. His wife was kicking him out. Neither of us had money to do anything but play tennis; no work in the summer for teachers. But we were there to cheer him up, pretend that life, for others, was pretty slick, that... that... like the movie star, he, too, could lick the "Big C". I don't know what we were there for. But we came, we saw, and we were conquered. We were etched forever on this terrible Grecian urn, standing there, Sikes and I, frozen with no words of cheer upon our lips, looking into Freddy's one good eye that was full of mists and shadows and frightening questions, an eye that looked through us and beyond.

Getting the nerve to go and see Freddy was one thing; getting out gracefully, saying goodbye was another. Sikes and I would catch each other looking warily for an exit line. Freddy knew this and he would try to smile with half his face, hold up his vodka glass to the fading afternoon sun, twist the glass slowly in his hands; then a deep silence and Sikes would say, for I was paralyzed, surprised by gloom, "The battle-axe is waiting for me to go to the store. Don't ever get married, son." Something inane like that. And then we would almost leap to our feet in relief, and say our flat goodbyes, and edge out the door with a poorly-worded promise to come again, knowing that very likely, there would be no again. And out into the dying sun we'd go, and the air and the scent of lilacs in the yard would hit us both like a blow in the face.

I remember the last time we came there, Freddy had placed himself at the top of the stairs to wave a limp goodbye, and as we padded down the stairs into freedom, he had shouted or mumbled something down to us. We waved back, but neither one of us quite heard him, and it wasn't until later, at a bar, Sikes asked me what he had said.

"What could he say? Death is ugly, and death is truth, and that is all we get to know," I said.

"No," Sikes said. "This silent form, dost tease you out of thought. Like eternity. That's what he said."

ALL MY DARLINGS

March 3—Wednesday: The first thing I saw coming onto Mother's floor level were the parents of a waxen-faced, tow-headed girl who were wheeling her around the hospital halls. The parents themselves were like snapshots caught in frozen mobility by a cheap amusement-park camera. The young girl had dead-fish eyes with horrible cocoa-brown circles under them; she was more like a statue than flesh and blood, more like death incarnate than a patient, and I felt this to be a sinister omen, and I rushed to Mother's bed, down the long, antiseptic hall, but she was sleeping quietly with an I.V. tucked into her thin arm, and after that I never saw the sick girl again—or her parents, thank God.

March 4—Thursday: It all started as a joke, and when Mother asked for her glasses, Ruthie popped her big black plastic frame ones on Mother's dainty button nose, and she didn't know the difference for she had her eyes tight shut the whole time. And then she asked for writing paper, in that hollow whisper, and I made a quick grab for a magazine on her night table and made it rustle like stiff stationery, and Mother, only half-conscious, half-delirious from the effects of double pneumonia said: "I must write. Now! I must write it now or I won't ever do it."

And then she let her thin arms sag at this and her head spilled back on the pillow, white hair against the white pillow, like snow sliding into snow. But then Ruthie spoke up in bright, cheery tones: "Don't worry. We will write all your letters for you. We're the best letter writers in the world." Then, when there was a pause in Mother's ghastly, heavy breathing, I asked: "Where shall we send the letter?" And Mother whispered in those cavern-like tones that were to grate on my ears forever, "To...to... everybody," she said. "Send the letters to everybody—all my darlings."

Then slowly, like water trickling out of a faucet, she began to dictate to Ruthie: "I'm sorry to cause you all so much trouble, and...and..." Then Mother made some wavery, scrawly motions in the air near the magazine that I was holding for her, and then she slipped back again like some white orchid against the snow of her pillow, and whispered again to us: "I must write to them now, or I will never do it."

Both Ruthie and I began to cry a bit after this. The "them" were just Ruthie and me, and our sister Louisey who lived an expensive air trip away in New Jersey and who had a sick child on her hands: three "darlings" all told, and hardly worth writing to. It struck me then, too, that Mother hadn't talked so much since her fall that sad night in her apartment. It was the job she clung to, I suppose, in hopes that one of her "darlings" might return from our feckless travels, from our wild plunges out of her nest, and come back to live with her like in the old days. Or perhaps she clung to that miserable job, in that dungeon-like safe deposit vault, for her own sainted independence. And then came the month of big snows, and the janitor of her apartment told us later, after we had gathered Mother's broken body up and shipped her to the hospital, that in the days before her fall he used to watch her start down the street to the bus stop and her job, she being 83 at the time, and walk a few steps and lean against a snow-covered elm simply exhausted by the effort of trying to walk in the drifts.

March 9—Tuesday: Mother is in a double room at the hospital, sharing it with a Mrs. Pinzenhasenham, or some such incredible name, and Ruthie and I snickered at the sound of the name. Mrs. P. is a dumpy, bull-dog of a woman of about forty, who, too, has pneumonia and she coughs a great deal, great wrenching coughs, and we despair of our Mother having the strength to cough up such phlegm for she will have to do so in recuperative stages of the ailment. Today, Ruthie tried to force some eggnog down Mother's throat. One of the pressing problems is that she won't eat anything, and her hands fluttering like aimless birds as Ruthie forced the drink on her.

March 19 — Friday: Mother is recovering some, but her mind is wandering now, like a ship without a rudder in a misty sea, and Ruthie forever crying bitter salt tears at Mother's bedside, mainly about our sour joke about the letter writing, but also about Louisey not being at Mother's bedside to spell Ruthie who is to go home very soon to her impatient husband. Ruthie and I talked today about getting Mother a private room, but the expense is prohibitive and then, too, funny Mrs. P. does keep watch over

Mother after a fashion, and rings for the nurse if she seems to be in trouble.

March 20—Saturday: We moved Mother from the hospital to a nursing home today. Her doctor, a thick, lumpish man with hard blue eyes shining behind spotless steel-rimmed spectacles, said he frankly was surprised that someone Mother's age could lick double pneumonia. In fact, he confided to us then, that he didn't expect her to survive the ambulance trip to the hospital for Ruthie and I had finally arrived at Mother's apartment late at night, and she was whisked away in 18-below zero weather, the ambulance lads bundling up Mother as best they could, but still they couldn't entirely help the shock of that biting cold in her lungs.

The nursing home, luckily, is just across the street from the hospital, and thus the ambulance fee was modest—only fifteen dollars, which Ruthie dug up from somewhere. The nursing home looks something like a cheap, flimsy motel—all pink and blue pastel shades, reminding me of Hardy and his remark about gay times matching gay architecture, but "alas, if the times be not gay...."

March 21—Sunday: Mother seems melancholic today, staring listlessly at the floor when I came into her room, bearing my poor gifts of magazines and lemon drops. I guess the problem is: how to keep her flagging interest alive in this narrow, box-like, trivial world. And I don't know how. Ruthie is gone home now to her world of demanding husbands, and I'm stuck with the problem. Sometimes when Mother is listless like this I think I would like to hawk sleeping pills throughout the home. "A hundred dollars a box," I would cry. "Pills to put you to sleep forever!" And I would get a hundred takers in half a minute.

April 5—Friday: This place, this nursing home, which by the way, I have grown to hate, erodes people. There is a woman here; Chaucer would have described her in one word: *gentilesse*. And she did seem high-born, or perhaps high-falutin', as they say here in the West, but no, not quite that. She was simply quiet and well-mannered, and under a bit of a shock that her family had dumped her here. She came crippled with rheumatism in her wheel chair, but she sat up straight and was meticulous in her dress and person. She wore conservative black or grey tones usually, and an imitation diamond choke collar to hide a wrinkled neck. But all in all, she was very neat and proper and she reminded me of the Englishman who dresses for dinner in the steamy jungle. She, like my mother, kept pretty much aloof from the others, wheeling smartly down the shiny pink halls to the dining room for her meagre suppers. But I saw her later on, and she had become "nursing-homeized"; there is no other word for it. She wore a sleazy cotton house dress, stained with food. She slumped in her wheel chair and her hair was uncombed, and there was a faint trace of urine in the air about her. This is all some sort of minor tragedy, I suppose, that goes on every day in nursing homes throughout the land. But this particular cheer-and-drab-all-at-once place would pull anyone down, just as the tropics with the heat and the green sameness finally gets to the Englishman. Why dress for dinner, after all, to sit with the old codgers, these dull drabs? And so you conform; you slide into the jungle muck.

April 10—Wednesday: Talked to the superintendent of the nursing home about the poor food and poor nursing attention Mother seems to get. This thing is a huge chain operation like the supermarkets; the shrewd businessmen are cashing in on the old folks' problems. But this smiling, toothy-faced superintendent has handled Mamma's Boys before. I mean, I told him that my mother had said the nurses "thought more of keeping the beds looking neat than they did the inmates," that they were "thing orientated" and certainly not "people orientated" (although I made this last phrase up for Mother doesn't think along these lines, or at least wouldn't be guilty of using this academic diction). But this head administrator, or whatever he's called, smiling a salesman-type smile meanwhile, kissed me off neatly. And I guess he's right about momma-boy types; the world brushes them aside all too easily. He argued that my mother had been pampered, and the more I bring food to her from the outside (Mother had complained she was often hungry), the more she will be dependent upon it, and thus feel free to dismiss her dinner trays, which he said were "adequate from any dietician's standpoint."

And I suppose he is right, but any institutional food for old folks, concocted mostly of jello and mush, served either too hot or too cold is for birds—not for people.

April 15—Monday: Mother needs her nails cut and I cannot spare the money to bribe one of the nurses to do so, as this is not part of their routine, a routine which evolves around pills, bed pans and food trays mostly, and so her nails grow longer each day, and no one around, since Ruthie went home, to cut them. Mother and I play like we're Chinese, and I don't cut my nails either, and we compare them for length each day, but the game soon tires.

It is a beautiful spring day today, and I had hoped Mother would go for a ride, or rather, a push in one of the home's rickety wheelchairs, but she is feeling especially feeble and scarcely wants to sit up high in bed—a bed designed by Procrustes for it is too large for her wasted frame, and she keeps slipping down toward the bottom and her grey, pasty face looks up at me sadly. All the faces seem grey here, greyish blobs set against the cold facts of pink and white bedspreads... all hulks as those described in Heine's poem: wrecks come at last to shore, battered in this pink, bedspread sea, their sails gone, their hulls rotten, and they slosh gently against this soft shore until they die of boredom. One hulk is moved out to the cemetery just as another creaks into this port. Although today, as if to deny Heine's poem on old age, I heard a story that put a chill in me. In a room down the hall from Mother's is an old, old, old lady: 104 years of age, so they say here. Her daughter, age 70, used to come every day to read to her mother who is mostly blind. But then she, the daughter, died quite suddenly of a heart attack, and the old mother is still alive, lying in her bed like some determined lump, and she can't quite understand why her faithful daughter doesn't come to read anymore.

April 23—Tuesday: Came this morning early, which is against the rules of the place, but Mother was involved with bed pans so I left flat. My timing was poor. Bed pan users of the world arise, you've nothing to lose but your dignity! Oh, if Mother only had the strength to walk to attend to these personal affairs. This frantic ringing for the nurse who comes too late, alas, and so Mother dies slowly, bit by bit, in this embarrassing way. How much better to go down dramatically with a *Titanic*. And I see myself here soon enough, sitting in my own wallow, waiting for my pan or my plastic dinner tray with its dull, plastic-tasting food.

April 25—Thursday: Today, Mother talked of her apartment again. We, of course, had to give it up. I think often of her dainty apartment, too, with all her prints of the French Impressionists, plastered every which way upon the soft brown walls, and the ones by Walt Kuhn and his chalk-white clowns, and the ballet dancers of Degas, fragile and pretty as Mother herself in the days gone by. And I thought, too, of Mother's strong black coffee, and when, earlier in the hospital when she was sick most unto death, we held out this apartment to her, with all it contained, as some goal she should get better for, come back to. And we lied in our teeth for we had to give up the apartment almost on the day she went to the hospital for the rent was way too much, and then later we had to pay high rent at this nursing home with its lacklustre food and its weak coffee, and we couldn't pay both—all her darlings, I mean. She never knew, and still doesn't know, but I guess that she senses it, that her apartment is gone, and her furniture and goods scattered in Ruthie's home, and Louisey's far home, and my small rooms. But I keep up the talk about the apartment, and she does too, as if it remains solid as the pyramids.

"When you get back to your apartment," I say, "you can have your coffee as strong as you like, and your pictures will all be there, and the little brown dressing table with its heaps of magazines and hairpins, and woman-clutter, and your telephone where you can talk endlessly to Aunty Jill like you did in the past." I don't quite say all this, but most of it. And thusly I keep the past alive for her, a past contained in this messy apartment, but it is all she lives for really, a shining grail held before her weak, fading eyes—and this maybe gives her courage to live on.

But, of course, the day is soon coming, for she is getting better, that I must tell her the apartment is long gone. I will have to get across to her, gently, that she really has no place to go home to, not even my dingy rooms, and that maybe she is trapped forever in this horrible home with indifferent people to wait upon her, people waiting to shirk their duty and let her go unbathed, unfed, and unattended for her mind would be wandering and she wouldn't quite know or care too much if she had her bath or her pills, and no one around to watch over her if I get ill.

May 1—Wednesday: One of the nurses, middle-aged, I suppose, or fortyish, with big black eyes is always snotty to Mother; lets her wet her pajama pants and is slow about a change, and we look daggers at each other because she knows I know she is sloppy about her job. But then today, I saw one of the orderlies pinch her hard upon the cheeks and then, when she drew away, standing in the hall in front of a few inmates, he pinched her intimately on the buttocks, and a warm flush spread over her face, which I guess is a tip off, about something, and I wonder if she's passing it around and if I might give it a try. Surely this young snip orderly has pinched her long and often before. On second look, she doesn't seem too old, maybe late thirties, but it is so awkward to go from conversation about my mother's wet drawers, to buttock pinches in the hallways; I'd better not try. But the nerve of that young snip to be so bold right in front of several of the old ladies who pretended they didn't notice. But I feel certain they got some sort of a tingle from this sex play. I know I did, and me not married and no one to go home to.

May 5—Sunday: Arrested for speeding again, going away from the nursing home. I have yet to be arrested for speeding to the home. I suppose this means something Freudian, but I don't care. The police have some new radar junk that nabs the unwary motorist—damn their gadget souls to hell.

May 10—Friday: Mother is confused about time and dates and she thinks I come every day, but mostly I come three or four times a week. My "affair" with the pinchable nurse gets nowhere. She does not smile in the halls, nowadays. If I only had the nerve to stroke her fanny as we pass by. But maybe one must have the soul of an orderly to summon courage to pinch a nurse in broad day-light, in the bright, bright halls of this nursing home where everyone and everything is finally exposed—or so I would guess. And me? I have the soul of a Mamma's boy, the nerve of a mouse, and the dreams of a March wolf. And yet, Mamma's boy or no, right now I couldn't bear sharing my small rooms with Mother— not at least until she gains control of her bowels.

May 11—Saturday: Today Mother said in a loud voice: "The Vienna quartet is the finest in the world," and this upon my first entering her room before a word of greeting had been exchanged. I think she meant the Budapest, but this was said, I suspect, to impress her new room partner who is stone deaf, and no doubt tone deaf, and wouldn't care much if the quartet was the best in the solar system.

May 14—Tuesday: Mother either talks about the "Vienna" quartet or Moses, repeating over and over that Moses never lived but was just a "beautiful story." And then her sermon on the non-existence of Moses is often interspersed with: "They gave me cold pancakes again for supper... waugh!" Although I found out later, after discreet inquiries among the more friendly nurses, that her supper that night had been toasted cheese sandwiches. But any food that Mother doesn't care for turns out to be "cold pancakes." But it may be her eyes that are failing along with her taste buds. Speaking of "friendly" nurses, I saw the pinchable one in the hall just as I was about to go home, and she had her coat on ready to leave and I said, "Can I give you a lift?" Lord knows where I got the nerve. But she looked me up and down as if I was a worm and said no thanks in a super-flat voice. A bit later, I saw her slide into the hot rod of this young orderly; he is young, vigorous, and full of vinegar. She'll get pinched plenty, I thought, before she gets home—which is what she wants anyway. This all depressed me terribly and when I got to my rooms I gobbled down two sleeping pills to forget it all. I mean, it's not much fun to be a mother's lad at my age, and I must soon be shopping for a mother-substitute, I suppose, if I ever can get up the nerve. This Miss Pinchable would be ideal: near forty, like I am; firm, like I am not; and I could lean on her I'm sure. Better still she could swipe sleeping pills for me.

Saturday—May 25: Raining out, and I'm very depressed today. I sit by Mother's bed wondering how long we can both stand it for this home is much like a prison to us both. Old people look so uncompromisingly terrible with their teeth out, and their eyes watery, and they all sit in a circle in the main entrance hall and stare at me when I come in, resenting my "youth" I'm sure, and their eyes cry out to me: "I was young once, too. I could walk as fast as you, eat anything, say anything—hear anything! And now I'm in a wheelchair, staring at the walls and waiting for meal times and pill times—and you will too, soon!"

May 28—Tuesday: I brought her bacon today, keeping it hot, somehow, by putting it between my legs as I drove over. And the food did give her sudden energy, and she began to talk in her high, ghostly, whisper of a voice. She talked today of what had been and what might have been, and she was so wound up that she wouldn't stop talking for one second, until she began to cough and cough, so I walked out quickly so that she would rest. But part of me stays always in that grubby little room with the linen not too clean, and the floor not swept.

June 4—Tuesday: Mother walks about a bit now, and she told me that an inmate stopped her in the hall saying: "You'll be alone, too, with us pretty soon." And then this old crone cackled like the witches in *Macbeth*, and told her: "They can't keep it up. My son once came every day, like yours. Then he came once a week. Then he came twice a year—Mother's Day and Christmas. Now he only comes once at Christmas. They all drift away." My mother answered her, shouting: "We all live too long, but my son will come every day! Every day—do you hear!" And then she hobbled away, her head held high.

June 8—Saturday: After I left Mother today and went back to my rooms and I thought then would I soon be like those sons who forget their vegetable parents? For the months seem to inch by one by one, and my mother and I, we float on this strange bedspread sea to nowhere. Will I not fail to come at last and sit on the prow of this frail ship of her life? And will that old crone be right at last, that I will fail to come back? Sometimes in dreams I see myself running, running, and not coming back to this hateful home and the old witch in the next bed, Miss Humalong, who in this dream I see clasp my mother in her withered arms, saying: "There, there dearie. I knew it would come to you. We all warned you. They all fade away. First, it's every day. And then it's once a week on Sundays. Then, only on holidays, peering at you as if you were some ghost from outer space. And they pat you a bit. No kisses anymore for your breath smells, and they leave little gifts that you have no use for, and then they go away, hurriedly. And then it's never! Never, I say! Oh, they write you sometimes, and your eyes hurt, and you can't read their letters, and just maybe one of the nurses will read them to you, but they read them hurriedly for they've so much to do, and that is all. You have a few letters in your hand and silence, utter loneliness."

And I see my mother then sobbing bitterly in this old hag's arms, and what am I to do? I can't come here forever and ever, like an oaf, bearing up my mother on this cruel bedspread sea. I must find some life of my own, somewhere...

June 21—Friday: Tonight I brought her some cheap canned spaghetti and meatballs (cost 30¢) and she is so grateful, or pretends to be, for she tells me they served pancakes and potato chips for her supper, and so tonight while I sit by her bed, she smacks her lips over this horrible canned mixture I have brought her, and no doubt she thinks if she doesn't pretend to like it I will run away. And God! Sometimes how I would like to just drift away and leave her with the soiled sheets, and her bed pan, and her false teeth in a glass by her bed, for I was not meant for this, this last guard duty at the death of an old woman. But there is no one else to come now that Ruthie has gone back to her husband, and Louisey with her sick child. And to leave her now would be like tearing off a leg, like deserting someone in distress on the high seas.

June 23—Sunday: Today she grasped for me with her cold hands and said: "Your hands are so, so warm, and my hands are so cold." And I pat her and lean over to kiss her and I am about to say, "I must go now for I have been reading to you for all of 50 minutes now," but her eyes turn to me like stricken dog's eyes, and she says, "Not now, it's too early." And my eyes say in reply, "But the old fool in the next bed has to get her sleep, and we can't keep her awake talking about Moses and when Daddy was alive and we had some money, and there were trees on our lawn in Denver and how you used to get up at five every summer morning to water these trees for it was bad to water them later in the day when the sun hit them, and I can't keep up this banal conversation with you..." And all this my eyes say to her. But with my mouth, I say: "I will be back tomorrow for another ride on your bedspread sea, my warm hands clasping your cold ones as we ride and bounce on our way." Mother laughs at this and says, "This is not time or place for poetry," and then I ease out.

And who could have foreseen this terrible boat trip? And I remember the night I prayed in the park in Denver that you might live when the doctor said you had double pneumonia and didn't have a chance, a prayer, and I asked our mountains for your life; the same mountains, I suppose, where Moses came down symbolically with his stone tablets, and my prayer was answered, and I do have your life, but not much else for you, my darling, are an empty shell, babbling on this boat while I try to steer to... to... where I don't know.

THE FLYING DUTCHMAN

Alfie and me could see the flares a long way ahead on the desert and I said I bet it's one of those damn acid hauling trucks we been passing run outa gas, and Alfie said if it was one of them he wasn't gonna stop and help none and "t'hell with the jerks." But then I was driving and I knew we would stop. "It's like the law of the sea," I said to Alfie. "You help a sister ship in distress, acid or no acid."

And pretty soon we were almost there and I began to shift down like I was in a racing car for we were carrying ten tons of furniture or so, and then I eased her into low and pulled to a stop over on the shoulder. But we could see it didn't seem to be truck trouble: no flats, no burned out brakes smoking. Alfie called out hello, for the truck's lights were on, shining down the road, and in a minute as we walked toward the truck with its funny, hour-glass behind and its narrow wasp-waist to carry the acid, we could see two men standing in the road, and Alfie called out hello again in his scratchy voice and said, "You need any help?"

But there wasn't any answer, and we could see then that the two men were squared off as if ready to fight, and like a fool I pushed in between them and said, "what's up?" And one of the acid men growled back, "heaven was up," and they didn't need any help.

I backed away then and Alfie and me stood there watching anyway, for maybe a good fight would develop, and Alfie was a bit touchy after watching the roads all day and needs to take part in a roughing up to get his circulation going again.

But nothing happened. The two men just stood there in the light of the flares, and then after awhile one of them, a small stocky man, said, "Son of a bitch. Let's forget it. I didn't see the car. I'm just chicken." And the two drivers without a word, got in their cab and left me'n Alfie just standing in the road with our own truck turn indicator flashing on and off.

I felt kinda spooky alone out there in the desert with the sand cliffs looming up in the flares and our headlights and all, and so in a quick minute we snuffed out the flares and climbed back in our diesel and went on toward Horsetooth Bend, but not before Alfie said: "I tole you and I tole you, anybody that drives one of them acid trucks is a plain slob, and I'll swear I'll never talk to nobody of that kind again, so help me if I'm starving."

"They get more money," I said.

"And so does the TNT carriers, but who ends up with all the money? The widows."

We never thought no more about it then and stopped talking. Riding the long desert stretch from Four Corners to Horsetooth Bend—it's 97 miles of pure desert and slow going because of the curves—you don't feel much like talking, only watching the road and how our lights would hit the cactus and a stray jack or two skittering before us. Pretty soon I told Alfie he should climb back in the bed above the seat and get some sleep, and he said, no, a bargain's a bargain. "On this damn stretch we sit up and keep each other company, that's all. You sit up coming back this way, and I'll sit up going now."

It wasn't long before we passed the acid truck on a long, slow grade. "Acid drivers just sorta crawl along," Alfie said as we pulled ahead peering into their cab. "I seen one that turned over. And I mean they carry some kinda hydrochloric acid, or some undiluted acid, and this junk poured into the cab through a break in the window—and that's all boy! Them guys were..."

"Don't tell me," I said. "I got a bad stomach as it is."

It was still dark when we rolled into the truck stop at Horse-tooth. We should have kept moving because we were behind schedule, but mainly we stopped because of the counter girl, Dixie, who waited on the graveyard shift and wore that low-cut uniform with no slip under it, and Alfie always thought he'd get someplace with her if we stopped a couple of more times. And I began to kid him about Dixie as I parked the truck and we walked to the front of the place. "Alfie," I said. "Look, boy. Down boy! You ain't never gonna make a haul on Dixie. You been saying this about every waitress on this run, and you ain't had one out to hold hands, let alone plan them big things you plan."

"I'm just biding my time," Alfie said. "I work kinda slow."

"You work slow all right. It's three years now on this run and I ain't even seen you play footsie with a cow."

There was nobody in the cafe at this time but two truckers playing the pinball machines, and we ordered coffee and sweet rolls, except Alfie quick changed his order to milk and rolls because it was going to be his turn to sleep until we hit Elko. And then we just sat there watching Dixie swing her hips around for our benefit, and pretty soon I kicked Alfie and said, "Now, boy. Go get her!" And then I laughted aloud. Just then we heard a truck outside, and Alfie said it's the acid boys because he's got a good ear for motors, and in a minute the two men came in slamming the frail door against the black night.

I could see them better now under the lights. There was the short, stocky man, the one who had done the talking, and a tall, dark-haired thin man dressed something like a cowboy in blue jeans and a jacket with a mean scowl on his face and eyes like tar pits.

And before these guys can order their coffee, Alfie speaks up, because after driving all day and night he doesn't care what happens sometimes, and says: "Well, ain't you mugs a couple of sweethearts now. I thought out on the desert back there we was gonna have a funeral." And I kick Alfie and whispers shush up because I don't like the looks of Tar Eyes. But the short, stocky driver doesn't seem to take offense, and he says, "I'm sorry about that." And then he shuts up sudden.

And we all start eating our food, but the tall thin driver, as we gulp down our harsh coffee, finally says, sneeringly: "Well, my partner here is kind of bugs, see. He keeps seeing this old car in the desert."

"I saw it," says the partner, his faded blue eyes glinting. "But we were yapping about whose turn it was to sleep. I mean, it was my turn to drive all right, but I like company on that long haul from Four Corners at night. I mean I want somebody awake with me through the desert."

"So you seen an old car," Tar Eyes said, and his voice grated like shifting gears on an old truck. "So what am I to do? Sit up all night and hold your blasted hand?"

The short, stocky man clenched his fists and started to get off his stool and for a second I thought we'd see some action, but Alfie jumped up trying to be a hero, I guess in front of Dixie or something and said, "Well, it is kinda spooky on that desert, and it's lonely, and..."

But then one of the truckers standing by the pin ball machines, who had been drinking this all in, came up to the counter and sort of grinned. "Thank Gawd, somebody else saw that car!" I gulped down some raw coffee and the story began to pour out into the room.

"I'll swear I thought I been drinking," the trucker said, "and you can't drink on this job for very long, that is. You know, I seen it just a month ago. You know the place where you make that long turn past Four Corners, and here comes this car, an old touring car. One of those with isinglass windows that button up. And I swear there was a damn lady in it and some kids, and she had on this old duster, you know, that grandma wore maybe. And before God and a big White truck, this car passed me, and me doing about 70 downhill! I hear this *ponk-ponk* sound of a horn, and here this thing comes by me—maybe some old Locomobile, and some guy with goggles, so help me, is squeezing this big horn, ponk-ponk. And I says to myself with Sam here sleeping up in the cab, I says no guy can pass me in an old car, and I let her out see, and I'm deadheading with nothing in my trailer but some rocks for the old woman's rock garden, and I can go pretty fast."

The trucker stopped to get his breath then, and I looked him over. He was a grey little man with steel rim glasses—not the kind you'd think would dream up stories to pass the time in a lonely truck stop. He reached over my shoulder suddenly and took my cup of coffee and took a swallow with a wink at me, and then he started talking again. "But anyway," he said, "I couldn't get near this thing. It was gone by me like a damn ghost, and then it began to fog up in the desert, mind you, or maybe it was a mist, and the road seemed slick and all, and I slowed her down. But I thought maybe I was dreaming."

"Speaking of dreaming," Alfie said then, "that reminds me of the time I was driving my girl home one night..."

"Shut up, Alfie," I said. "You know you ain't never had a girl, and besides I heard this story before."

"Well, we're gonna have bed time stories." This from Tar Eyes, and I quick got up from my stool because I'd seen a leather knife sheath showing inside his jacket. Alfie's eyes clouded up at this crack from the tall thin one, but he didn't make any move, mainly because I'd slipped in between the two of them. But then Alfie smiled and I knew he'd simmer down. Just then, too, Dixie came up to the counter and said, "Look what I got!" And as we all sat there drinking our drinks she slammed down a coin and spun it on the counter.

"Look at that," she said right to Alfie. And Alfie slow like he is, took it up, but Tar Eyes, impatient and fast-moving, reached out and grabbed it. "It's a nineteen-ought dollar or something," he said. "Well, it's a damn old coin."

"You're damn right it's an old coin," said Dixie. "Worn right down to its nub."

"My little brother will go for this," Alfie said, and reached over deliberately and took the coin from Tar Eyes. "He collects coins, you know. He's a numan... a hypnotist or something like that. But this one's so old I can't make out the date."

"Where did you get it?" I asked.

"You guys talk about seeing ghost cars on the road," Dixie came back. "I've never heard truck drivers talk so damn much in my life, and me a woman can't get a word in crosswise anymore. You think you got troubles! But I'm on the overnight shift in this joint, see, all alone. No other joint until Elko, and if I ain't a greasy spoon they all came right in here last night to eat. I'd like to die and nobody here but me and Fatso asleep in the kitchen."

"Who came in here?" Alfie asked. And there was a sudden hush, and Dixie's eyes widened.

"Who came! Why the people in that damn ghost car, that's who! And you better gimme that coin back," and Dixie reached out and grabbed it away from Alfie.

"Look," said Tar Eyes, "I'll give you five bucks for the coin." Dixie smiled a wide smile and showed two gold teeth. "Okay! Fair enough!"

Tar Eyes slammed a five dollar bill on the counter and eased the coin out of Dixie's hand, putting it in his upper shirt pocket.

"Well, it won't bring you no luck," Dixie said, and Alfie guffawed at this, but Tar Eyes came back quick: "I ain't looking for no luck," and he stood up suddenly and I thought maybe he and Alfie would have a go at it right then and there, but Dixie sort of calmed them down with a look or two and began telling her story about the people in the old car.

"I woke up Fatso quick enough when they left and he heard the car pull away making its funny sound, and so I ain't crazy—and I had this coin, too, which helps me think I ain't been dreaming."

"Well, for Gawd's sake, that's a relief," the short stocky partner of Tar Eyes said. "I was all spooked up about them, but now I'm thinking they must be some of those antique car nuts with a hot motor in their buggy just for a gag."

"Antique car nuts, hell," said Dixie. "Lemme tell you. These creeps were the genuine article. The father comes in first, see, and there's five of them. The old lady in a duster gown and a big hat, and three little kids all bundled up every which way. The father is blowing the little kids' noses, and he says, 'Now we can't have too much to eat. We're running low on funds.' And I couldn't believe my eyes! They just stood there in the center of this room getting warm I guess. And then one little girl goes to the toilet and I follow her, 'cause the john don't work right. And I'm in the can with her and you know those old-fashioned cotton stockings like your grandma wore, I ain't seen them kind for years, and this little girl was trying to hook up the garters and the strap was old and it broke and I gave her a safety pin, and her crying and sniffling all the time."

"You're joking," Alfie said, "you're making all this crud up so we'll drink more coffee and get kidney trouble."

"Lissen," Dixie snapped. "You guys want this story or not!"

"More bed time stuff for the kiddies," Tar Eyes said. And at this Alfie stood up tall, and said, "Go ahead and tell the rest of her."

"Well, I'm in the can, see, trying to fix this little girl's garter strap, and she had a funny dress on like I seen in the movies once, and this kid is thin like a rail. Honest, I was afraid to touch her for fear she'd break in two, and I finally got her stocking pinned up, and I said come on out now, and she said she didn't ever want to come out, and she began to cry and she put her thin little arms around my neck, and come to think of it later, I didn't feel no weight around my neck and I tried to tell Fatso this, but he just laughed.

"Well, we come out the can and the rest of them are all sitting at the counter, and I set them up with coffee and milk and donuts for the kids. And while they were eating, the old man pulls out an old linen map and spreads it out on the counter, and then he asks me where 'Ninny-vah' is or some such town, and I came back I never heard of the place. And then, ye Gawds, the Mother joins in the fun and says the map's no good anymore, and for father to ask 'the servant', that's me, for directions.

" 'Father,' she says in a high flutely voice, 'aahsk the servant where we ah.' "

"But old Dad right away says no she wouldn't know the place

or Gomorry either. All the time I'm staring at them, my eyes as big as dish pans, thinking maybe this is some movie company, making a movie and trying to kid a poor waitress. But no, they go on talking for real.

"Pretty soon the Daddy says, and I quote you from memory: 'But we must go on. It will be light soon, and I know this is the road. The road will turn off at the church and we shall be there at last and there will be an end to all this.'

"I chimes in at this and says, 'Lissen, Buster, they ain't been a church in the desert for 300 years unless you mean that little Indian mission that's nothing but a heap of stones down the canyon past Elko.'

"But Mother doesn't pay any attention to me, and she says, and get a load of this, in her high flutely voice: 'There is no end,' or some such jazz. And then she went on: 'We have been driving since the start of time, and you say there is a home to go to, and there is no home, only this car, and ourselves, and that is all except the dark road that goes on and on.'

"And then the old man comes back at her: 'But there will be an end, soon. I promise.' And then there was no noise at all—really weird, except the wind and the crying of the three kids."

"You're making this all up," Alfie said again. But he didn't say it very loud.

"Cross my heart," Dixie said. "I remember every word, like it was a movie. And then the old man bundles up the kids and he starts to pay me for the eats, and I say it's on me, but he says 'we will have none of your charity' and as they all troop outa here, the kids crying and carrying on, Dad sings out: 'Now it's just over the next hill. A stiff upper lip for all of you, and at the next town we will find the right road.'

"And my Gawd, they all go outa here, and it's like I'm dreaming, and I quick wake up Fatso in the kitchen, and the slob wants to know what's eating me, and I says, 'What's eating me for hell's sake, look out the window there, and he does and he says it's one of them old cars and what am I so excited about, and then we hear the noise the motor makes—sort of a pop-pop sound, I don't know. And this jars old Fatso up some, and he runs to the door and looks out and me with him, and by all this time all we can see is a lantern—a *lantern* for God's sake, going off down the road."

"Well, I give up," Alfie said then. "I can't top a story like that."

The two truckers driving the acid wagon got up at this, the tall, dark one scowling. "Well, thanks for the story," he said. "Come on, Hans, we'll be hitting the road. But I still sleep on this stretch going through the desert, ghost car or no ghost car," he said.

The short, stocky man called Hans said in a funny way: "Maybe you'll be sleeping all right, but I won't." And the two acid drivers went out into the night, and I motion to Alfie we'd better be going, but he pulls me down by one of the pin ball machines and says he thinks he's got a line on Dixie, and I'm to go out and catch a few winks in the cab and he'll wake me up later.

"Lcok," I said to Alfie. "You maybe got a line on Dixie and it'll cost you twenty bucks, and we're kinda late now."

"Art," he says back, "You're jealous, and it ain't gonna cost me ten."

"I'll give you half an hour," I said, "and then I'm driving off without you." And then I went out and curled up in the cab.

So that's how come Alfie and me were a good half hour behind the acid truck going into Elko, and it was Alfie, I guess, seen the flares first, and the patrol car with its red light flashing way down the canyon where the old Indian mission stands, and I began to roll her fast and we were pretty soon there, although I hit the air brakes pretty hard when I seen the acid truck.

It was just getting dawn, and we could see the truck laying on its side with some of the cab crushed and the acid crud spilling out all over the road, and the patrolman flagged us down and said be careful of your tires, and I eased on past the wreck, put out some of our flares, and me and Alfie walked back, or tip-toed back, and there was the stocky guy, Hans, talking to the cop with a bloody handkerchief held to his face, and we didn't see the tall dark one.

"Take your time," the patrolman said to Hans, "and tell it your way." And this trucker Hans stood there in the half light of early morning with the patrolman shining the light right in his face. I could see now that he had a long cut across one cheek, like maybe he got cut on broken glass, and he shook some as he talked, and kept dabbing at his face with the bloody rag.

"They turned right into my truck," Hans said. "They came right over the divider, and I could see this guy with goggles in my headlights. And I'll swear he was grinning, you know, like he meant to do this, like he was enjoying it all. And there was a crash, I guess, and I swerved and my trailer jackknifed. I couldn't hear any noise when he hit me, and when the trailer jacked it slammed against the cab, but I jumped, and the acid spilled outa the seams...and he's still in there! We gotta get him out! We gotta!"

Hans' voice was rising to a scream now, but the patrolman was calm as stone. "In a minute," he said, "when the wreckers come and the ambulance fellows. I ain't gonna mess around in all that acid."

"Now, I mean!" Hans yelled, and made a move toward the truck, but the cop grabbed him and shook him some. "I . . . I . . . guess you're right," Hans blubbered. "But I . . . I . . . don't like my buddy just laying there, he . . ."

"How'd you get out so fast?" the patrolman asked. "I was driving and I smashed out the window and crawled through. Tom...he...he...was up in the sleeper, and I couldn't get him out when the thing jacknifed into the cab. When I saw I couldn't do...get...anything for Tom I...I...walked...I *ran*...along the barrow pit to see about this passenger car, and all I see is some junk, some rags and stuff as must have been lying there for years, and there was some dust all around. And then by the divider I seen a skull, and it was smiling at me, and I ran away that's all. And then I saw the ranch house over there and called you guys to see if you saw what I saw."

"Don't find no skull around here now," said the cop.

Hans was beginning to blubber again, and Alfie turned away choking because of the acid fumes, and he went back to our rig, but I stuck it out. After awhile Hans began to talk again with the patrolman writing some of it down on a pad. "You can look at the front of my truck where the car hit, but there's not a scratch on it. I don't know how to explain it unless I'm losing my mind. I ain't never had an accident before. My record's clean on this road," Hans said.

"Well, we're gonna give you a drunk test when we get you down at the station," the cop said, "but you saw something all right. I found this lantern or headlight or something. Anyway, it's brass and a place for a candle or a wick in it. Never saw such a thing. No wires no nothing."

Then Hans slumped over on the fender of the police car and began to cry like a baby, and I waited around until the wreckers came and the ambulance, but Alfie kept sitting in our cab like he was kinda sick. They got the dark one out, the one with the tar pit eyes—what was left of him. There was a big jagged gash on his head, and in one hand, burned black by the acid, he was clutching the old coin he got from Dixie; in his other hand he had a long thin knife.

Finally, I watched the ambulance men patch up Hans' cut face, and then I skirted the acid on the road and made my way back to our truck. There was Alfie all hunched up in the cab staring straight ahead. "Alfie," I said, "you two-bit Romeo, you and your cheap amours, I figure, saved our lives tonight."

"Cheap!" Alfie came back. "The little tramp wanted...But wait a minute! You believe the ghost car turned into the acid truck and it might have turned into us, if we just happened to be coming along?"

"I don't know what to think. But those other truckers talked about seeing an old car too."

"But lemme tell you something else," Alfie began.

"What?"

"Keep driving for awhile," Alfie said, "while I think this thing out."

There was a good ten miles of silence, and then Alfie began: "You know I didn't come back to the cab 'cause I gotta squeazy stomach. I seen acid burns and wrecks before."

"Yeh?" I said. "So?"

"But I ain't never seen a murder close up before," he said.

"Come down off it, Alfie."

"Now the way I figure that Hans and Tar Eyes had a long grudge. Some drivers grow to hate each other being cooped up in a cab all the time, and Tar Eyes carried a knife, see, and..."

"And you mean this little guy Hans waited until Tar Eyes was sleeping up in the cab and then he spun this $35,000 tank truck over in a barrow pit, and clobbered him with a rock or something as he tried to crawl out of the sleeper, just as the acid was reaching him?"

"Well?" Alfie said.

"Well, he did have a funny gash on his head."

"Yeh. And there wasn't no ghost car."

"I dunno," I said. "I like Dixie's story a bit better. There's an old coin and a lantern in that one. You ain't got much to go on," I said.

"I got this blood-stained rock with black hair on it," Alfie said. "I found this rock near the wreck. I mean it was in the barrow pit where I lit one of our flares, or I'd never noticed it. It does look a bit like a skull." And with that he held a roundish rock in front of my eyes for a second, and then threw it out the window.

"Maybe we ought to stop and get that rock for the police," I said, but my heart wasn't in it somehow.

"Look," Alfie said. "Acid drivers are all poison. Let's leave 'em alone. And then the coin. Now that I come to think of it, it was an old Spanish coin or something. Maybe 300 years old. Maybe worth... maybe worth..."

"Enough to bury the poor guy," I said, and we went driving down the canyon towards Elko. But in just a little bit I said, "Funny thing, Alfie."

"Funny thing, what?"

"Sometimes at night, especially in the desert, I get the feeling there ain't nothing but this road. There ain't no Elko to get to. We've been driving forever, and there ain't nothing else."

"Look," Alfie said. "We're going to get to Elko and we'll stop awhile, and I'll buy you five or six beers and we'll shake this whole thing off."

"It's a night that ain't gonna shake off easy. But I'll drink all the beers you can buy," I said.

ME AND WILL

I really never could sell much of my poetry until I began signing my "work" Will S. Shaekspir, which, by the way, is the true spelling of his name. But if I had it to do all over again, I never would have bothered, for the whole affair was more or less one long migraine headache, believe you me. On top of that, my ego took a brutal kicking around.

It all came about when some joker in the English department where I teach three sections of freshman comp and one small class in Shakespeare stopped me in the hall. With the usual sneer in his voice he said: "Say, Croaker, I see you haven't been publishing much lately, eh? Publish or perish—that's the watchword here!"

"Yeh," I came back weakly. "Any sage advice or anything?"

"Say, I got a great idea, Croaker! Whyn't you evoke the Heavenly Muse? That always worked for old Milton!" And away he skittered down the hall laughing his jerk head off.

And so, one dark smog-filled night, I did just that. I mean, what did I have to lose? I started out like Milton in *Paradise Lost*, "sing heavenly muse," and then I dropped a bat's wing and an eye of toad in a pot of hot chocolate, all the while reciting *To Be Or Not To Be* backwards. Then, throwing the decanter of my concoction into the fireplace, I said: "Make my Muse be Will Shakespeare!" And damned if it didn't work!

All of a sudden there was a puff of smoke and then there was this strange man in my study with those absurd puff pantaloons and frilly collars of Queen Liz's time, and Will, or this person, said: "Stand not on idle ceremony, for I'm here to do thy bidding," so I knew right away who it was. The only thing I could think of to say was: "Oh, Will! You're bald!"

He came right back and said, "What he hath scanted in hair, he hath given them in wit." I didn't recognize these lines, and so I said, "You're not something out of an LSD sugar cube?"

"Your words are some obscure," he said, "but in any event, I'm your heavenly muse. You said the proper magic words... ah...backwards. And here I am!"

"Well, I'm mighty pleased to see you, Will," I said. And then, without further ado, I outlined my troubles at the English department.

"Much ado about nothing," he said in reply.

"Men have died for less and worms have eaten them." And then I gave him my proposition. "If you'll write my poems for me, I'll sign my name to them—but you get all the money!"

"Well, I ghosted enough in my time, true enough. But to strip my words down to bare truth, ere it pains me," he said, "I'm not here because of any mumbo-jumbo evocation to any Muse. Heavenly, or the other kind. You see, I've been having a bit of a go up in heaven. That is to say, a gaggle of we ink-stained geese, myself, Herrick, Pope, Sam Johnson, and old Ben, always sit around in a celestial version of the Mermaid Tavern and talk. And lately they've all been picking on me. Jealousy, pure and simple, of course! Pope, that crabbed, wizened little man, said that lucky for me I was born in Good Queen Bess's time, or nobody would have taken my poems, and they go on and on. And I think it was Ben Jonson who wagered that if I returned to earth in these parlous times, I couldn't get published.

"I said: 'You're on, Ben!' And that fool Lovelace joined in on the banter. And so when I heard someone give Hamlet's speech backwards, an evocation, by the way, bad enough to make even Herrick turn in his tomb, I came back to you—although there be many other poets twixt heaven and earth I would rather have helped, verily s'blood!"

"Well, Will," I said. "It's not the will I want as much as the deed, and I'm glad you're here and let us make do with my second-best bed of poesy. Now, I've been working on this little verse of mine on smog, and it hasn't come out just right—and you can get to work on this right away, for I imagine when the cock crows you will be obliged to..."

"Smog! A dull, smack grey-sounding word, in truth! Oh, that I was born to put such a name to rights. An out-of-joint word for an out-of-joint time!"

I took Will to my window then. I live on the top floor of a lower middle class, high-rise apartment complex, and my tiny balcony looks out on the freeway and the factory district with its ever-belching smoke stacks. "Ugh!" said Will. "Sweet, sweet poison for thy age is Soot!" He looked for a time at the cars zooming past, and the smoke stacks, and the grey, grey smog that enveloped half the world, and turning from my windows in disgust, said: "No, I cannot do it! Back I will go to the fragrant wood smoke and ale-fumed rooms of the Mermaid and confess that I'm a twice-gulled fool. That I have been outwitted, out-connied by a Croaker, a veritable thin Cassius-like crow of a man...a..."

"Well, all right. I'll keep the money. And we, you use your name as you see fit. But mark you, Will, t'will not be easy to send in verse signed William Shakespeare."

"In the first place they misspelled me name all these dark and alien years. We will sign the work Will S. Shaekspir. And mark the a, e, and the p, i, r! And though this name be not wide as a church door, nor deep as a well, t'will serve. And now to this verse of yours on, ah, SMOG!" Will tripped the word not lightly on the tongue, but more like sand crammed in a crow's mouth. "In my day we wrote upon our fair one's eyes that were very like the sun, and today we test our quills upon some chemical mixture of carbons, alchemy, and soot concoctions! Ah, what a falling off is this! No! Perhaps it were better you had called on old Ben Jonson. But, I will do my best. Let's see what you've done."

"Speaking first of fair ones," I began, my eyes taking on a scholarly gleam, "how about first clearing up a few mysteries about the Dark Lady and the true author of *Pericles* and..."

"Stay!" Will commanded. "Surely half my fame rests upon these intriguing puzzles. Should they ever clear up, scholars would drop me like hot lead. Now to this poem of yours!"

Reluctantly I took out of my desk a little attempt I had undertaken two days before on the horrors of smog in our time. Imagine what a stew I was in to shew my verse to the greatest poet of the ages—nay, of all times! "It is a mere nothing," I stammered. "I..."

Will smiled indulgently. "What is't that you took up so gingerly? So like an asp to bite my Cleopatra?"

"An ill-favored thing, sir, but mine own."

"This! This is a 20th Century poem!" Will thundered. "The very rats, editors I mean, instinctively will quit such a leaky vessel of verse!" I cringed, and then Will smiled a bit more kindly. "Ah, Croaker, 'tis well you evoked the Muse!" He then read the first line aloud and we winced together: "I'm all agog, because of the smog. . ."

"Holy saints preserve us, Croaker! You don't need a Muse—

you need a complete construction job! A doctor, a carpenter, a mason, a physic, twelve magic charms, two hundred encantations, a philosopher, a bishop to say prayers, an alchemist and a sorcerer!"

"Please! Harp not on my shortcomings. Thou cans't not make a silk poem out of a sow's ear sort of verse, but let us try to make a virtue of necessity. Smog is what we try to breathe in this day and age and..."

Will held up his hand in an imperious gesture. He gave me one of those penetrating looks of his. He had the largest, the deepest and the blackest eyes I had ever seen. They were something like, well, a vacuum cleaner. They seemed to draw out of you whatever you were thinking, and leave you feeling wrung out and exhausted.

"Smog? Hmm. Well, Jonson said that true to our bet we, I, could not use any of my old themes. I'd have to write pure 20th Century verse. Hmm, well. Indeed, we will write a sonnet on smog!"

"Well, not a sonnet, Will," I said. "They've kinda gone out of style. A little free verse maybe, or some Imagist stuff?"

"None of my verse shall be free, except that some pay for it."

"Well, Will, as I explained before, I'm not interested in the money end of it. Nobody pays much for poems nowadays. But to keep my job I just have to have my name in print almost constantly."

"Now wait a blessed minute! You, we, are not to use my name on my poems?"

"Well, that was the basic idea behind my first evocation—I mean, I thought that was clear. You get all the money, of course."

"Money! Why a full purse is worse than a sow's ear at the heavenly Mermaid. Everything is free there! Food, drink, lodging. Would that old Falstaff had made it up there with me..."

"But...but..."

"Out upon it! But me no more buts, as Jonson would say. I'm down here on a wager, that even today in this 20th smog-ridden century, I can get my verse acclaimed on every tongue. How now that I should sign my heart's blood Leslie B. Croaker, or some dull-sounding, clunk-like bell of a name, as a bell in the tower of Old Bailey that has gone sour with age, like the sound of the cawing of a withered crow fallen upon evil times, like..."

like...S'blood! Words fail me!"

"Condemn the name, but not the bearer of it," I said quickly. "Please, let us fast to the marriage of our true minds, and not dwell upon this curse my father handed me, for after all, what's in a name?"

"Better a little chiding now, than a great deal of heartbreak later on," Will came back.

"Here, sit down at my typewriter," I said, "and see what you can do."

"Typewriter! What on earth! There may be many things in heaven and earth, dear Horatio Croaker, but a type machine is not in my philosophy. Have you not a quill pen, a beaker of ink and one of ale—and I will to work!"

I stood for a minute paralyzed, and then Will thundered at me: "Oh, base Hungarian wight! Wilt thou the ale-spigot wield! For if ale be the food of poetry, I must drink on and on!"

"Well, Will," I stammered, thinking on my meagre supply of 3.2 beer, "you sound more like Falstaff than the Bard, but I think I can manage some weak beer, but on my oath, no editor today would think of reading anything written from a quill pen! You'll have to dictate to me and I'll pound it out."

"Don't know if I can think with that cursed contrivance chattering at me. A dreadful invention!"

"We do not ride upon the typewriter; it rides upon us," I came back.

Will gave me a sour look. "Very well," he said. "Let us begin."

"What needs be done, best be done quickly," I said.

"Please! You do not know how I am ragged for my lines at the Mermaid now. Lovelace even threatened to return and erase the words upon my tomb. 'To Be Or Not To Be', he said he would substitute for the warning about my bones. And then add: 'No More A Question!'"

"The scoundrel," I said. "Stone walls were too good for him!"

Will paced around my room for awhile and then, leaning over my shoulder, he said: "No, let us put Dante into this poem on smog, for I gather quickly that one needn't travel very far these days to visit that dreadful bourne... "

"Where no man returns," I added quickly.

"Ah, yes. Well, something like that. Smog! Traffic accidents! Wars, poison gas, H-bombs! Let's bring old Dante back to the

20th Century, and end our poem with something like, ah, 'Aban-
don All Hope Of Air, Ye Who Enter Here!' It will make old Dante
twitch, I can tell you. He's such a surly fellow; he sits brooding in
a dark corner of the Mermaid, scarcely talks to anyone any
more—much like Dean Swift. Two of a kind—two misanthropes.
And along with Moliere they make quite a team, I can tell you.
I'm sure they're busy writing a play to confound all the Angels of
Heaven. Milton will be sure to censor it!"

"Milton!" I cried in disbelief.

"Oh, he's changed since DeSade's *Justine*, and a dozen more of
such ilk. He's trying to organize a heavenly Star Chamber; the old
Puritan blood came out and he is to burn his *Aeropagatica* in
effigy!"

"High time, I suppose," I said lamely. I was about to add: "Ah,
Milton, would'st thou were with us in this hour," but I thought
better of it. Meanwhile, the Bard kept striding restlessly around
my poor room, gesticulating grandly, stopping every now and
then to look gloomily out my picture window, quaffing all my
poor stock of beer. In fact, I thought maybe I should have sent for
Milton, who, I'm sure, was a teetotaler. Or then, perhaps,
Wordsworth. But putting in a call for old William would mean,
very likely, reciting *The Prelude* backwards, at which my mind
boggled.

But finally, before the cock crew, and my beer was exhausted,
Will dictated a beautiful anti-smog sonnet. In subsequent visits
to my room he penned, via my obedient typewriter, a long anti-
war poem, one on the horrors of subway riding, and a romantic
epic on our population explosion.

Well, I needn't go on and on with the rest of my winter-like
tale; I, of course, got fired from the English department. No one
would swallow the idea that I felt constrained to publish under
another name than my own. It is true, Will earned me a modest
amount of pelf, for despite the jibes of Jonson and Lovelace, the
Bard hadn't lost his magic touch. I mean to say, he could trans-
cend his age—something Sam Johnson, at least, must have been
very well aware of when he came in on the wager with the rest of
the Mermaid tipplers.

But my story does not end here. Broke, and out of sorts, I
conjured up Will one more time. I put it to him bluntly:
"Although the poems you wrote for me," I said, "have sold unto
twelve editions, poetry at best earns scant shekels these days.

And through all these monkeyshines I have lost a pretty good job..."

He cut me short: "My heart bleeds."

"But a play," I said. "A play's the thing to catch the purse strings of commoners and kings..."

"And what's more, there's movie rights to put things more to rights!"

"And TV and residuals! The wealth of Croesus shall be mine—ours!"

"Well, in truth, one thing has been on my mind all these dry and inconsequential times. One character of mine has pricked me to the heart and for him I have bled these whoreson years."

"Othello!" I exclaimed. "You've read about our riots at Watts and Detroit?"

"No, blockhead! Shylock! Browsing through your library I've seen the photos of your World War II—I mean the concentration camps. And the diary of that little girl, Frank. I'd trade my *Hamlet* for it! I'll rewrite the old play, but put it in modern dress, with Shylock as the hero. As for Portia, she will be the cruel mistress of Belchen or Dachau. Her quality of mercy will be strained, I can tell you, when she fashions lampshades out of human skins!"

"And what of Jessica?"

"That heartless strumpet shall die in a Nazi soldier's brothel for deserting her father. And as for Antonio? He'll be an SS spy, and the angered Jews will tear his heart out. They'll get their pound of flesh—ten times over, I warrant you!"

"The title? What's to be the title?"

"Why *The Merchants Of Munich*! Or...or...*The Monsters Of Munich*. What's in a name?"

"What, indeed," I said excitedly. "A gas-chamber by any other name would..."

"Reek to heaven!"

And so we, or rather he went to work. The play, of course, was a smash. It ran two years in London and New York; five years in Tel Aviv. I got ninety percent of all the royalties and skipped to Switzerland before the IRS could track me. I cached the swag in a numbered bank account, and left the academic life for good.

I sit here now, looking out over placid Lake Lucerne, and wonder sometimes about Will. I'm sure he's back at the celestial Mermaid now, sitting securely at his rightful place at the head of the festive board. "Ah, Will," I can hear Ben Jonson say, "Triumph my Britain, for thou hast but one to show!"

BUTCHERDOM

Then I spotted most of his little finger missing, more than just the tip, almost down to the last knuckle, and I knew it must be he: Arthur Caldwell Townsend. Of course he didn't recognize me, and I stepped up to the counter and ordered one pound of ground round, and he gave me a casual glance out of his watery blue eyes—eyes now needing thick glasses. And as he wrapped up my package I looked at the finger again. He had cut it off, or so the story went, while chopping a hunk of liver for a Mrs. Kleinhasen, or some such name; and in a fit of pique, or in a state of near hysteria, he put his finger tip, blood and all, in with Mrs. Kleinhasen's liver, wrapped it up; took her money and then fainted dead away behind the counter.

But he was like that; I mean, from what I gathered from mutual friends, for we were but acquaintances. I found out, second-hand, that he doggedly learned to play Beethoven's piano sonata in D Minor, despite the finger being gone, despite his starting the piano late at twenty-seven or so, long after his hands had stiffened working in the freezer cutting meat. From what I knew of him, it seemed part of his character to protest his butcherdom, to take part in the arts, and not resign himself to being pushed into a corner and made a butcher.

I did, once, hear him play the Beethoven: play it, if you'll forgive this expression, like a butcher might render it. I'd been invited to the house of a mutual friend, Dick Orrison, and he had a piano, and after a few drinks all around, Arthur Townsend was prevailed upon to play it. But just imagine, attempting that singing, rolling, D Minor work with butcher hands, with the little finger gone, or a useless stub. As I remember he got through the entire work, earnestly, pedestrianly, but he did play it: certainly some triumph of man's spirit over unfriendly fate and the liver-buying Kleinhasens of the world.

Now, as I looked at him as a surgeon, an internist, I could see he had liver trouble; very likely he ate rich foods in defiance of this ailment. That was so like him: defiant. Others in his family, and I imagined he had a big butcher-like family, had been able to indulge themselves on rich waffles, smothered in butter and syrup, or greasy doughnuts and French fries. And Arthur would certainly go on in life not being squeezed out of participation in anything, and to hell with the nausea and the jaundice. All much as Oscar Wilde is said to have remarked about the Grim Reaper: "Here comes that old bore, pretend not to notice him."

Pretend not to notice my finger tip gone, Arthur would say, pretend not to notice my jaundice, take part in this life with all cylinders forced into function, and be damned to you fates! For that certainly was Arthur's point of view—or at least, this is how I put together the puzzle-picture that is Arthur Caldwell Townsend.

Why do I remember him at all, for I haven't been back to our mutual hometown, Lincoln, for over twenty-five years? And why did I shop from store to store in hopes of bumping into him? Arthur and I really knew each other only by chance meetings at Dick Orrison's home. The Orrisons were all long gone from Lincoln, and perhaps I felt lonely or curious. Mostly I remember Arthur, not about the finger accident, or the *D Minor Sonata*, but for his wonderful anecdote about the fur coat and the zipper on his fly. And thanks to Arthur Caldwell Townsend, for many years in my party-going days, I owed what scant popularity I could muster due to my acting out Townsend's incredible experience at a movie.

You see, he had taken his best girl to a film—movies were but fifty cents in the not-so-golden days of the Depression—and they were sitting mid-aisle. Arthur drank fairly heavily then, I supposed to help wipe out the reality of butcherdom, and he had earlier excused himself to go to the men's room, and coming back, noticed that he had failed to zip up his fly. Next, in this amazing sequence of events, a woman with a shaggy fur coat of some sort had excused herself to pass by Arthur and his date on her way out of the theatre. Arthur, seeing his chance to be extra polite to impress his date, and to thereupon slyly zip up his fly, stood up, and as the lady passed by he quickly zipped up his pants.

Unfortunately, the zipper caught, or rather snagged firmly on the coat, and rather than rip out some of the fur, Townsend followed this woman out of the aisle, terribly close to her, indeed. And then they walked in step, up the long ramp to the lobby, the woman looking back apprehensively at this strange man who

was following her so closely. Arthur's date, meanwhile, sat angry
and puzzled at her escort's strange behavior.

Finally, the two zipper-joined twins arrived in the well-lighted
lobby, and the indignant lady screamed "Masher! Pig!" Arthur
scooted out a side exit in the confusion. Then, belatedly, he
found he had no money, and no stub to re-enter the theatre, and
although he waited an hour or so at the main entrance his date
never appeared—vanished apparently into the heavens.

Really, this was a comic tragedy, so Arthur explained, for his
girl had promised great events for later in the evening. She had
been very free with her knee during the movie, and if it hadn't
been for this whimsical fate incident with the zipper, wonderful
things seemed in store. As it was, Arthur felt the whole thing too
unbelievable to relate to a girl of this "ilk" is the way he put it, and
he never could quite bring himself to phone her and offer an
explanation or an apology. Thus he abandoned his quarry to the
luckier wolves of the world who are often, zipper-less, on the
prowl in movies and such fine places.

Well, with many embellishments and eye-rollings on my part,
I learned to mimic or act out this tragedy of Arthur's, and for
several years I fancied I was in modest demand at cocktail gather-
ings with my little skit about The Great Zipper Fiasco. I did,
shamefully, practice various facial expressions, and even
recruited my wife to play both the parts of Arthur's angry date,
and the indignant lady with the fur coat.

Thus I remember the Arthur of my youth, of his youth, and
now seeing this old, faded butcher who had doggedly stormed
his way through Beethoven's incredible beet field with his plow-
like hands and hammer-like wrists, who even now was very
likely defying an angry fate, an angry liver, or so I diagnosed, by
unflinchingly digging his grave with his false teeth—teeth long
ago, like mine, lost in these petty and unequal battles we all fight
against the gods.

I was very much tempted to say to Arthur Townsend as he
wrapped up my hamburger: "Would you remember a Michael
and an incident of a zipper?" But butcher Townsend looked so
grey, so yellow, and so tired! Why then bring back the past? Both
our pasts were best forgotten and stored away amongst Mrs.
Kleinhasen's liver package, and also along with that mean, heartless sonata Beethoven wrote to try the shallow souls of everyone

who thinks, foolheartedly, to attack the great arts with butcher hands, and alas in my parallel case, the great art of healing with a butcher-like mind.

I was tempted to say also: "Arthur, Arthur Caldwell Townsend, I do love you. I do think of you!" But what would this mean to an old tired meat-cutter, now defeated in life, I'm sure. And if I can, as a doctor, read lines in faces, Arthur must have lost a son in the last stupid war, and perhaps did grieve for a wayward daughter. I can see all that in Arthur's face—or do I mean my face has these tell-tale lines? But indeed, Arthur at least won his lines magnificently in the battle with D Minor sonata, a battle which would be struggle enough, even if you had all your fingers with two extra besides.

Ah, the finger! Could I but write a requiem for Arthur's lost finger, lost unto the last knuckle—for if in the Kingdom of the Blind the one-eyed are in control, in butcherdom the one-fingered lads perhaps are lowest paid. But then they have learned to survive by learning caution. But, as I have said, in his pain and hysteria, Arthur Caldwell Townsend wrapped his finger up along with Mrs. Kleinhasen's liver, all in one bloody package. And Mrs. Kleinhasen, dear soul, no doubt cooking without her glasses, fried Arthur Townsend's finger, along with the liver. And Townsend, who had fainted and was revived, and then rushed to a doctor, heard some terrible words from his physician... even as I have said terrible words to my patients. "Get me back your finger, quickly," this doctor said, "and we'll sew it back as good as new."

Did Arthur Caldwell Townsend know Mrs. Kleinhasen's home address? No, he did not! But it was found in the phone book, hours too late for a successful graft, if I'm not mistaken. Although I don't know for sure, but I do imagine that the finger had been fried along with the liver and a batch of onions. Perhaps indignant Mr. Kleinhasen spat out the nail, cuticle and all, and had said: "pghagh!" to his wife. "Bad liver this! Change your meat market!"

Or then, again about Arthur's finger, perhaps it was fried to a crisp and not noticed. But let us imagine Arthur's consternation, his hand swathed in linen and tape three inches thick, and his pounding on Mrs. Kleinhasen's door, and she coming to the door, adjusting and setting her glasses on her nose to see who it was who was knocking so frantically, and poor Arthur stammering: "Do...do you have my liver...I mean, my finger!" And then further chaos and consternation on both Arthur's and Mrs. Kleinhasen's part when the bitter truth was learned—a truth made more bitter for he had lost both the finger and the D minor work.

I'm sure when Arthur's garbled message at last soaked through to the Kleinhasens, they both flirted with the idea of suing the meat store, and perhaps they did. But in any event, Arthur's finger was gone beyond redemption by the medical arts, and a bit later, Arthur, child of misfortune, was let go. For who wants a butcher around with no baby finger, a butcher who is obviously accident prone and a touch dramatic? A strange butcher, too, who was apt to whistle Mozart or Beethoven sonata sections on the job. Sadly, there was no insurance for Arthur, and no kindly employer who would keep him on out of pity and compassion.

But of course, there were other butcher shops—many of them. And if your father happened to be a butcher, you were too. And in the Depression Days, if you married young, you had to keep your job, grimly, for there were no other trades to switch to, and no money for music training at an academy. And so Arthur Caldwell Townsend was swept irrevocably into butcherdom, and along this bloody way lost a beautiful bed partner, and lost one finger necessary to play a sonata with any bravura and dash.

And there, I do suppose, but for a quirk of mindless fate go I, and perhaps you and you. I, too, lost a lovely girl at a movie. The film, *Smiling Through*, starring Leslie Howard or some lump-in-the-throat-style actor, induced me to cry uncontrollably. And when the lights went up, I was terribly ashamed, for my date, who I mistakenly thought was looking for masculine strength, and perhaps machismo, grinned at me askance out of tearless eyes. Once in the well-lit lobby, I hid my red and tearful face into my handkerchief, and walked away from her, for I felt all had been lost, much as Arthur Townsend had decided not to wait endlessly in front of the movie for his date to appear and had driven home alone to drink and curse at fickle fate.

There, at this meat store, some twenty-five years later, I felt a strong kinship with Arthur. I, too, Arthur, I wanted to say, lost a lovely girl and thinking back on both of our lost dates, seen through this haze of old age and watery eyes, they both seemed fairer than Helen of Troy, or that wiggly, voluptuous Alisoun of

Chaucer's tales.

I came back several times to buy meat from Arthur Townsend. I tried to whistle the second movement of the D Minor, but I found this impossible to do. Then, very likely, I reasoned he wouldn't remember the tune, or would fail to recognize my shrill rendition. I did have an old record of Arthur Schnable playing it, and I toyed with the overly-dramatic plan to put the piece on my tape recorder, and then, as I ordered a pound of liver, casually snap on my portable player, and drench the butcher shop with one of the music masterworks of the world. Then (and only in my imagination), I would catch the shock of recognition in Arthur Townsend's washed-out eyes, and in a burst of joy, he would clasp my hands in some bond of disappointed brotherhood and pretty soon, as our friendship renewed itself, I would suggest a few cures and medicines for his liver ailment, and all would be right and ship-shape for Arthur Townsend towards the tag-end of his raw, meat-like life.

But then... but then in a more hesitant and sober moment, I was fearful that it would be more like his luck, and my poor luck, too, to intensify his ailment rather than cure it. With this spectre dogging my thoughts, I resisted going back to the meat store for many months. Truly, it must not be a good plan to dabble into anyone's life, to bring back the comic-painful past.

But finally, before I decided to give up my medical practice and move away from Lincoln for good, I stepped once again into Arthur's meat store. But he was not there. I asked a man behind the counter about Arthur's whereabouts. "You know," I said, "a tall man with blue eyes, a finger missing."

"He's no longer with us," was the reply.

For quite a long time after that, I felt terribly lonely in Lincoln. My wife dead, children gone, my practice dwindling away. And I asked myself why my belated interest in this mere acquaintance. "What of me?" I asked myself. I, too, have been in the butcher shops of the world. And I have lost more than the tip of my finger along this route, Arthur Townsend. Yet, we are brothers, and why didn't I speak to you? And I will search for you in the meat shops, but you will not be there. For no one will want a jaundiced butcher who has been fried in the fleshpots, who has lost his finger and has, worst of all, been crushed by the *D Minor Sonata*, a work that, among other things, can bring into terrible clarity the possibility that your life has meant nothing, nothing at all.

THE TENNIS BUM

Sam Tianella came each summer to Cranston's ostentatious country club when they held the state tennis matches, and the grounds were thrown open, rather reluctantly, to the general public. In his early years of tennis-watching, Sam had arrived dressed in immaculately-white tennis ducks and sneakers, but his racket, hopelessly battered, gave him away, for it was hardly up to tournament caliber.

Actually, Sam detested the game from the start, but his white togs allowed him to mingle with the others, and he felt he was being accepted as a contestant: a defeated duffer wiped out in the early rounds, but still accepted. Thus he would stroll around the entire club, watch the golfers putt on the beautiful emerald greens near the courts, and stop at last by the pearl-white swimming pool to stare at the inexpressively lovely, tanned bathers: young girls so trim of figure and smooth of skin that it was almost a pain for Sam to watch.

And for a time, before established club members looked closely at Sam, he too, was of the very rich, lounging in a sway-back chair, idly watching the swimmers or players in preliminary matches, not obliged for once, in the uncomfortable vicinity of the rich, to fetch and carry.

Sam carefully saved up his money each year for the tournament, and arranged his vacation time—he was a waiter in a large downtown hotel—to coincide with the tournament dates. He allowed himself so much for the spectator's entrance fees, and quite a bit more for the food, for the members always seemed to be eating or drinking, or at least just about to eat, and the food was lavish and expensive. Negro waiters dressed in white denim coats ran here and there with huge trays of crabmeat salad, iced tea, and cool drinks, and there were incredibly large chicken or turkey sandwiches with heavy white meat spilling out of thick slabs of bread in wasteful splendor.

And so, at the beginning, Sam bought and ate, and bought and ate again, and tipped the hustling waiters extravagantly, and for the moment he was a bonafide club member, basking in the same warm sun, ogling the young swimmers, or the female tennis contingent in their tiny ruffled shorts, smiling and nodding at them, and the girls in turn, would look away quickly with a puzzled feeling, certain that they must know him, and yet not quite sure he was of their set.

This masquerade worked fairly well when Sam had been young and presentable with his black hair slicked back, and his trim tennis pants repressing the bulge in his spreading middle. Funny, Sam would think then, as he sat in a canvas deck chair, a long drink clutched in his short fingers, his seedy racket slung carelessly on the lawn beside him, how much he had hated tennis as a boy, and now here he was each year, his nose virtually rubbed in the white lime and clay. As a student in high school he had felt tennis players were, well, sissy, and beneath any he-man's notice. He had played baseball himself, clumsily, but with a passion. Later on, when he had begun to drink fairly heavily on his days off from the hotel, he had had to give up the sport for his reflexes were poor. He often dropped the long, high flies that came to him at his lonely post of center fielder, and the resulting boos from the crowd tore at his heart.

But then, his baseball playing days quickly over, he became a fan, an *aficionado* of the sport, and spent long hours by the radio, or went at night to the free softball games at Cranston's city park. It was just here, sitting in the rickety stands watching the game, yelling at the umpire, a beer in one stubby hand, that Sam had had an enormous feeling of ennui and detachment that led him, at last, to a kind of sport snobbery. He had read in some pocket-book a diner had left at his table, about the "goggle-mouthed Brooklyn Dodger fan," who drank beer, who liked pornographic pictures, bowling, and B-grade musicals, and suddenly he saw himself in this new, unflattering light, and knew he must find a new sport to go with this new sense of superiority—a superiority born of a chance encounter with a popular pocketbook on social customs.

Tennis had occurred to Sam almost instantly. Hardly anyone watched tennis tournaments; no one in his small circle of friends had ever played the game, or indeed, given it a passing thought. How to set himself neatly apart from his friends, from this screaming, ill-mannered crowd in the soft ball stands? Why the answer was simple enough: take up tennis. To take it up, not seriously, but as a spectator, for running around in the warm sun in those delicate white outfits still didn't quite appeal to him. But he reasoned that he could be an aloof, urbane spectator, clapping politely at each successful overhead smash and stinging serve, and gently murmuring protests on doubtful line calls. And then, too, he as a tennis fan, could rub shoulders with the well-to-do, and this seemed after all the most important to him.

Therefore, Sam had begun to seek out tennis games at the public parks and eventually, through the sport items in the newspaper, he found his way to the Cranston country club and the state matches. But as the years went on, and as he grew older (he now admitted to 45), his tennis clothes seemed shabbier, and his sneakers not quite so pristine. His tennis ducks especially, once so white and brave in the Cranston sunlight, were lacking somehow in the latest style touches as the years went on. Then, too, most players had switched to brief shorts, and Sam with his knotty, hairy legs had been reluctant to follow. Worst of all was his racket, a square-headed instrument that must have been in use in the early 1920's.

His wife, Lydia, nagged him about the sports expense. "Why don't you go back to softball?" she asked. "It doesn't cost us a dime." Sam would shrug and smile a tolerant smile at these remarks. "You just don't understand," he would answer. But fashionable or not, Sam still came, a bit defiantly now, to the matches each summer. After all, he reasoned, the club was then open to the public, and maybe a beer-guzzling, erstwhile baseball fan was just the thing to give the tournament a little extra zing; or rather, a bit of down-to-earth shading that Sam felt was sadly needed in the almost sterile, starched whiteness, the almost stifling atmosphere of gentility, that now began to set Sam's teeth on edge.

Sam would stare now quite shamelessly at the bathing girls who, plainly visible from the tennis stands, swam and dove in the pearl-white pool next to the courts, stare sullenly at the girls grown ever more golden and nubile, and the bathers in turn, would smirk angrily and turn away from his stares, for now his clothes so obviously advertised that he was an outsider.

Then, too, due to mounting expenses at home, plus Lydia's nagging, Sam was obliged to buy the cheapest of club foods—hot dogs, beer and soda pop—and this by itself labeled him immediately as a mere tennis onlooker. This feeling of being an outsider was really more than Sam could bear sober, and he now would attend the matches quite drunk, usually on beer, and sit in the cheaper seats in the broiling sun, and quite oafishly ogle the women players, and not watch the men champions at all—players who repelled Sam with their young, supple limbs, their swift movements, and their defiant youthfulness.

Sometimes, watching the swimmers, Sam would think then of his wife Lydia: dumpy Lydia. He had married quite young. Lydia was a quiet, drab girl who had worked as a waitress with Sam at the hotel, and they had had, rather quickly, two unspeakably drab children: two girls, who to Sam's oft-jaundiced viewpoint, seemed vague, shapeless blobs of flesh topped with pigtails and glasses. At the country club, though, Sam would shut his family out of his mind (at the start of Sam's tennis fever, he had sharply rebuffed his wife's attempts to accompany him to the tournament), and pretend that some of the incredibly lithe and golden girls were members of his family. That wispy blonde thing, sipping ice tea in the shaded center stands was his wife, and the two lovely, dark-haired boys sitting at her feet were his own sons, and his whole inconsequential life as a waiter didn't exist; that he was a successful stockbroker, and spent whole days at the club, playing bridge for high stakes, downing endless whisky and sodas, eating rich food, and casually watching young athletes scramble in the sun for a white ball.

But then at sunset, his daydreaming over, Sam turned prosaically into a pumpkin, a waiter and erstwhile baseball fan, and he would shuffle drunkenly out of the club grounds and make for the tram bus and home. Once home, with some effort, he managed to shut out the scenes and sights and smells of the club: the tinkling glasses, the supple brown thighs of the swimmers, the dark, careless eyes that had known so little of disappointment and despair, and he would wrench these pictures from his mind and heart until the next summer, when he knew he would be sitting in the stands once more, drunk, more defiant than ever.

In Sam's younger days he had tried, chameleon-like, to assimilate, to blend into that atmosphere of wealth and idleness. In fact, in the first few years of his tennis-watching, he even went so far as to take up tennis as a game in his own sort of maddening, desultory fashion that would infuriate his chance opponents. It was, at that time, cheaper to enter the gates as a player; the singles' fee was only two-fifty, and if you were knocked out in the first round, as Sam knew he would be, then your player's tag permitted you access to the grounds and all the matches, whereas if you came as a paying spectator, you were charged three dollars each day of the week-long tournament. Thus, Sam, dressed either in white, ankle-length ducks, and later, and more incongruously in tight, sausage-like shorts, and wearing cheap thin-looking tennis shoes, would play in the first round, his old butterfly racket going *twang, thud* at the smartly-hit balls.

Upon rare occasions, during his active period, Sam would actually manage to punch a ball back over the net somehow to the utter amazement of the gallery and his opponent. He was really, at these times, the laughingstock, the unwitting clown of the tournament. Red of face, Sam would slouch after the ball, hitting wildly—so wildly, in truth, that the careening ball would sometimes strike a startled spectator in the stands two courts away.

But most of the time, instead of any frantic stroking, or unseemly lunges, he would play with an irritating air of condescension, as if to imply that both the game and his opponent were far too inferior to bother with. And at the end of the match, with a score of 6-0, 6-0 against him, Sam would leap clumsily over the net, grab his stunned opponent in a wild and exaggerated hug or embrace and say either *c'est la guerre* in an absurd, twangy American accent, or, "That's the way the cookie crumbles, eh, Tootsie?"

Then he would go happily to the club's magnificent locker rooms where he would luxuriate half the afternoon in the steam showers, and then swaddle himself in the large, soft Turkish towels furnished by a Negro attendant.

Later on, in the second era of his tennis enthusiasm, and as he began to drink heavily, even this half-hearted gesture of "playing" would be too much for him, and he would merely stand, alternately on the odd and even sides of the receiving court, and make no effort to return the ball. And when it was his turn to serve, he would tap each ball deliberately into the net. Then, after but a few games, he would default, mumbling something about his "bad knee." Still, he was privileged to attend the rest of the games as a "player." The club tennis pro did approach him once, after a rather petulant and loutish exhibition on the court, and said something to the effect that, "if his *game knee* gave him trouble, would he care to call lines for one of the quarter final matches?"

This Sam readily agreed to do, and he did it so slovenly, so ineptly, that once a woman player, in a fury, flung her racket at him. Sam, laughing uproariously, walked off the court and took a seat in the shaded, reserved section of the stands, saying quite loudly, "Carry on, old girl, carry on!" He was asked to leave then, by an usher, but he immediately became so rude and surly that the usher retired in confusion, and the whole matter was more or less dropped as play continued with a new linesman.

The very next summer, in a ruling seemingly aimed explicitly at Sam, players out in the first round were required to pay admission for subsequent matches; that, or else serve as linesman and referees. Sam, obviously too tipsy or indifferent for these assignments, was now obliged to pay admission fees. This meant, more than ever before, that he had to buy the cheapest food and drink, and to sit in the bleachers in the hot sun, and all this labeled him as an outsider. This meant, too, that Sam grew ever and ever more sullen, and to "get back" at the club, somehow, Sam would now stare quite shamelessly at the young girl swimmers or female tennis contestants, so much so that they were obliged to grimace angrily at him, or turn away.

Sometimes, months after the state tourney was over, and he came off the night shift at the hotel, Sam would engage his wife, Lydia, in a conversation about the wealthy. "You don't know the rich like I do," Sam would begin, and smile a secret smile as though he had been initiated into some mystic rites of wealth, and he would then go on to elaborate on how they dressed and their manner of ordering servants about. Lydia would answer: "Well, of course, Sam. You wait upon them all night long at the hotel." And Sam would become angry at this and say, "No, no! I don't mean at work! I mean at that... that tennis club when we are equals and I can observe them in... ah... less... well, you know! I mean at *play*, not at the hotel! When they're relaxed you get to see what they're *really* like!"

Lydia, sensing a violent argument, would agree quickly on all his comments, and with her jaw agape and her crooked teeth showing in a twisted, yet pleasant smile, she would say, "Yes, Sam. I'm sure you're right about that."

After his long harangue on the habits of the rich was over,

Lydia would gather her two girls in her arms and retire to the kitchen where she would cry softly at the strange change that had come over her husband.

Each year, as it became more of an effort, more of a duty to go to the games, Sam began to hope that someone would help him make a scene, and he would be banished for good from the club grounds. He often envisioned a smooth, smiling club manager, dressed in a white summer tux coat and dark slacks, approach him and mention that, "as it was quite obvious he did not come to watch the tennis games," staring meaningfully at the bare legs of the swimmers nearby, "would he please leave this instant!" Sam then had rehearsed in his mind a retort for this that would make his eviction a dramatic certainty: "Well, if your girl members are gonna dress and act like cheap sluts, they're damn well gonna get stared at!" Then, timing his exit, he would spit a magnificent blob of tobacco juice on the manager's white shoes and walk out, head high.

But alas, no one ever approached him, or reproached him for boorish conduct, although now in the bleacher seats he was a familiar figure, and everyone would sit as far away as possible from him so as not to hear, for one thing, his loud belches born of beer and peanuts. In the unshaded stands, too, Sam began to treat the games as he would have baseball games years before, yelling vociferously, clapping loudly, and booing the decisions of the linesmen. Failing in these attempts to make himself obnoxious in the stands, he would often stumble out in the middle of a set, many times causing a tightly-strung player to delay his serve, meanwhile, and then wander the club grounds much like some ghost or apparition that people would stare through and around, but never quite at, and at the end of the heart-breakingly long hot afternoon, he would slouch dispiritedly to the bus line and go home to Lydia and the girls.

Each year it was more like an illness, a prolonged pain, for Sam to attend these matches; it was an ordeal to be gotten through with one starched dazzling white day followed by still another and yet another. And on the last Sunday afternoon when the last mixed doubles finals had been played, and the tournament slid to a stop, and Sam walked, for the last time again, the five long blocks to catch his bus, it was as if a knife had been pulled from his side.

It was one summer after a particularly trying afternoon at the matches that Sam struck out at his wife, Lydia. He had been as boorish as possible at the games that day, and had followed two young girl swimmers around, smacking his lips noisily, and saying loudly, "Ho, boy! Wha' the youngsters are wearing now! Diapers with brassieres! Diapers with brassieres!" But even this attempt at vulgarity had no effect; he was simply and completely ignored. He came home that late afternoon, tired, weaving unsteadily from too many drinks, and Lydia, unfortunately, met him at the door of their four-room flat. She had just taken the two girls swimming, and was still in her suit, a rather modest one that adequately covered her bulging frame.

"How . . . how did it go today?" Lydia greeted him.

"Slut!" Sam yelled in answer. "No wife of mine is gonna dress like them stinking whores! And our daughters, too! You shouldn't . . . you shouldn't . . ." Sam aimed a feeble wild swing at his wife at this point, and began to cry. "Never in my house!" he yelled and stumbled out the door.

Sam spent a good part of the evening drinking in a bar. When he came home the bedroom door was locked. He made a tentative tap on the door, but the two girls screamed at him: "You leave our mother alone, you dirty drunken pig!" He slept on the living room couch then, and when he awoke late the next morning, Lydia and the children had moved out, bag and baggage. Sam thought then of sending a telegram of apology to Lydia, care of her mother in Elkhart, Kansas, for that's the only place she had to go to, but he never got around to it.

Drunk, he went the very next day to the matches; the finals were on, but mercifully Sam was turned away at the gate with the excuse that all seats had been sold. Somehow, he killed the next four hours skulking around the neighborhood of the club, walking, cursing, muttering to himself about what he should have said to the gateman, drinking from a pint of vodka he had in his back pocket. When it was quite dark, he again approached the club grounds. No one was around, and he slipped in past the gate and made his way to the tennis courts. There, on the center court, which in the moonlight seemed to sparkle in white purity, Sam relieved himself, both bowels and bladder. Then he walked to the edge of the pool and on the pearl-white tile, near the diving board, he smashed his empty vodka bottle.

"There! God-damn them!" he said aloud. "There! That's what I think of their stinking God-damn sissy white pissant tennis game!" When he reached the corner where the bus was to stop, Sam was sobbing uncontrollably.

Three days later he had a telegram from Lydia. As he suspected she had gone home to Elkhart, but she would come home if he promised to behave. He telephoned her then, long distance, apologized profusely, and they were soon reunited. A week or so passed and when his domestic life had settled back pretty much into its old routine, Sam haltingly asked Lydia's permission to go to a softball game at City Park. "Yes, oh yes!" Lydia said excitedly. "Please do, Sam, and tell me all about it when you come home!"

In the fourth inning, on a close call at home plate, Sam stood up unsteadily, a beer clutched in one hand and yelled: "Kill that son-of-a bitch *Empire!*" A woman, sitting next to him, unconcernedly nursing an infant at one naked breast, laughed delightedly. "Yeah, man," she hollered, "kill the creep!"

Sam turned to her then. "Lady," he said, "you're after my own chubby heart. Lemme buy you a beer. Two beers!"

THE BURNING BUSH

"Mrs. Zofar, take a letter please, to ah...ahem ...God."

"Do you have his new forwarding address?"

"Mrs. Zofar, levity is out of place in this office. We are being paid to write a letter to God, and it is a matter of integrity and an act of charity, Christian charity, that we do so. The posting of the said letter, thank God, will be solely in the hands of my client, Moses J. Thistlewaite."

"Moses J. Thistlewaite! Now I know you're joking!"

"Thistlewaite is an old New England name. Quite a few settled out this way. And as for the letter, Mr. Thistlewaite before his...ah...illness, stated that God noted every sparrow's fall, and that he will thus pay attention to every letter sent his way, no matter how small and unimportant."

"May I ask, then, when and where did this sparrow, Thistlewaite, fall, and if we are to post this letter in the spot where the sparrows customarily fall?"

"As you transcribe the letter, all will be made known to you. Not clear, but at least known. And as I said earlier, the posting of the letter is in the hands of my client. Or rather, his wife."

"Very well. Two more questions. Can you collect a fee from a client who habitually writes letter to God?"

"The fee has been paid in advance; I was not born yesterday. However, lest you should think I'm unprincipled, this letter is written in the spirit of emotional therapy, as suggested by doctors, head shrinkers, attending my client."

"Very well. Now as to my second question: what is the salutation?"

"Dear God should be adequate. It is simple, unpretentious, and to the point."

"Very well, then. 'Dear God'. Or maybe, 'Ye Gawds'!"

"Yes. Dear God, semi-colon. Or rather, colon. My client, Mr. Moses J. Thistlewaite, hereafter to be called, the client, or Mr. Thistlewaite, of Rural Route 2, Mountain Home, Idaho, would like to call the following matter to your personal attention, colon."

"New paragraph?"

"Yes. On the 23rd day of May, in the year of your highness 1958, Mr. Thistlewaite, or rather, the client, states that a singular occurrence took place upon his farm, to be exact, in the south 40 section with frontage bordering upon Gopher Creek. Here, the client reports, he was examining hail damage to his spring wheat and he happened to glance upwards and to the left, and noticed that one of his choke cherry bushes, lining the banks of the small stream, seemed to be on fire, paragraph."

"Listen, Mr. B. Is this a gag, or something? I've got a lot of serious work to do out there. The accident report, and..."

"Mrs. Zofar, need I point out that everything we do in this office that brings in a fee, is serious work?"

"Boss, if you don't cut it out, I swear I'll call the Bar Association and expose you, or..."

"The state bar group already knows of this undertaking."

"Well, then I'm going to phone your wife and tell her you made a pass at me."

"I will then phone your husband and tell him that you made a pass, verbal kind, at me."

"Ha! My husband, for your information, would only laugh and say that if an old bag like you can get a pass, you'd better accept it and be thankful."

"I was thinking that is just what my wife would say, only of course, she would say 'old goat'. Now where are we?"

"Taking a letter to God about a bush being on fire, so help me."

"Yes. As my client, Mr. Thistlewaite, moved across the field to investigate the fire and smoke originating in the vicinity of the choke cherry bushes, he reports hearing a rather pontifical voice exclaiming, and we quote: 'Moses! Put off thy shoes from off thy feet, for the place whereon thou standest is holy ground.'

At this, the client reported that he spoke up sharply: 'Ain't nothing holy about this land, stranger. Got it from Tom Eliphaz, the son of a bitch, for two'n a quarter an acre.'

And Mrs. Zofar, by the way, better put a *sic* in parenthesis just after the word, 'ain't.'"

"Sick!"

"The Latin, s-i-c, of course, Mrs. Zofar. If God or someone *should* read this letter..."

"Good grammar ain't gonna help you or old Thistlewaite much

with God."

"Well, ah... let it pass. Now where were we?"

"Two and a quarter an acre. Son of a bitch."

"'Take off thy shoes,' said the voice in rather ominous and booming organ tones.

'It's too damn damp this time of the year. And who are you to shout orders, anyway? And while I'm on the subject, what's the big idea of smoking up some of my best choke cherry bushes? They'll be ruined for jelly making and my old woman...'

There was a great flash of light at this last remark, the client reports, and then there came a clap of thunder so loud it shook his hat off. But my client alleges that he stood his ground, and then the following conversation took place, here transcribed as accurately as possible in view of my client's present mental and emotional condition:

MR. THISTLEWAITE:—All this blustering around ain't gonna get you anyplace with me, stranger.

VOICE:—Venture not to excite the anger of the Lord.

MR.THISTLEWAITE:—I'm the one to be angry around here. Holy ground is it? From whose standpoint? Either all this land is holy around here or none of it is. That strip down by the railing ain't fit to plant cockleburrs in. Sell you the whole thing back for just what I paid for it.

VOICE:—Ah... take off thy shoes...

(Mr. Thistlewaite reported that the voice seemed to lack conviction at this point. The client here reported that he sat down on a tree stump and lit his pipe.)

MR. THISTLEWAITE:—If you're really the errand boy for the Lord, like you must be, you might tell him I got a lot of things to take up with him. No sense him coming down here and ordering me around at this late date. I never asked to be brought into this place noways. Fact is, my folks had a different end in view when I was in the early process of getting born. My getting born at all must of been a mistake, that's all. At least, according to my old man who spilled it all to me one night when he was drunk—the time he lost the north section when the damn mortgage came due.

Well, I got shoved into this arena, and it's been fight, fight all the time. It's bad enough without taking anything extra. Who started this mess, anyway? My only son dead from polio or some blasted thing. My old man dying all twisted up with pain in his gut. Not me it wasn't. Try this holy land business someplace else.

VOICE:—(Weakly now) Take off thy shoes...

MR. THISTLEWAITE:—And another thing! Remember the time Sarah was sick and the tractor busted down right at plowing time? Well, I called on your Lord good and often then, didn't I? I plumb wore out my knees begging on the ground for Him to send a little rain, too, and what did I get? Not a sign from anybody. Just duststorms, I got. And so now He sends someone to burn up my choke cherries and yammer about me taking off my shoes.

VOICE:—The ground upon which you stand...I mean the bush whereon you...

MR. THISTLEWAITE:—If this ground is holy, it's me, Moses J. Thistlewaite, that made it so. I watered it. I plowed it. You can't just drop down here anytime and tell me my ground is holy. You should of seen it before I came. Cactus and stones mostly.

VOICE:—You mean...you mean to say you're a Moses J. *Thistlewaite*!

MR. THISTLEWAITE:—Yep. That's the monicker. Moses J. of RFD 1, Mountain Home, Idaho, U.S.A.

"The plaintiff now reports..."

"Plaintiff! Hold on, boss! Is Mr. Thistleburr suing God for being born!"

"Hmm. I see your point. Of course, let's stick to *client*. The client now reports that the voice said: 'I beg your pardon,' and then there was a great wooshing sound, a clap of thunder, and all was quiet. The smoke and the fire had disappeared, too, from around the base of the bushes.

Mr. Thistlewaite reports that he said, 'Oh, to hell with it all,' and then he went back to the barn and began milking the cows. It was not until a cow called Bessie stomped upon my client's feet during the said milking, that he noticed his shoes were gone.

'They're gone! Just plain gone!' my client reported he cried. Then he ran back to the bush and raised his fist to the sky. 'Bring back my shoes! Bring 'em back, I say!'

It was not until just then, my client asserts, that he recalled the Exodus chapter of the Bible. A cold sweat broke out upon the body of my client, apparently in a reaction to the enormity of his impertinence to a messenger of the Lord.

'My God, what have I done!' my client called out in genuine

contrition and remorse. And then, he was reported by a witness, a Mr. Tom Eliphaz of a neighboring farm, to have run around his choke cherry bushes for a space of two hours or more.

Some time later, my client's wife, Sarah, reports that Mr. Thistlewaite was found by the hired man, babbling over and over to himself, the following words: 'My shoes! My shoes! Oh, what have I done! What have I done!'

The aforementioned hired man, a Mr. Aaron Bigsby, now of General Delivery, Grangeville, Idaho, stated that he carried Mr. Thistlewaite up to the farm house and then he and Sarah, the wife, put him to bed. Mrs. Thistlewaite states that she brought her husband a glass of hot milk and that he seemed to feel better after drinking it."

"Now really, boss, come clean!"

"Mrs. Zofar, we've been asked by his psychiatrist to write this letter for him. And that's as *clean* as I can come. So, to continue. The following information on my client now comes from Mrs. Sarah Thistlewaite. She reports that her husband apparently made a complete recovery from this 'seizure.' He returned to his farm chores on May 25 of 1958, and everything seemed to go along just as usual. On June 16 of that year, however, Mrs. Thistlewaite reports that the hired man, Mr. Bigsby, found my client leading his herd of milk cattle back and forth Gopher Creek, driving them with a long, hooked stick.

'It's the Red Sea! The Red Sea!' my client is alleged to have shouted at the hired man. 'It's the Red Sea and I'm getting them out just like the book says. This place wasn't nothing but cactus and sand before I came. Now look at it! Now look at it!'

The hired man then reports that my client grabbed him violently by the arm. 'Looky there! Looky there!' Mr. Thistlewaite shouted then, 'It's all milk and honey now! All manna from heaven!'

Mr. Bigsby reports that Mr. Thistlewaite then fainted and he brought him up to the farm house and he was put to bed. From that day on, and for three weeks more, my client was acting so erratically that he was institutionalized, and that as a consequence of his confinement, the Thistlewaite farm fell into disrepair.

My client, since September of 1958, has made an almost complete recovery, as testified by competent medical authorities, and he has gone back to work on the farm; however, the winter wheat crop was a total loss (as the hired man was not capable of hand-ling heavy farm machinery), and thus Mr. Thistlewaite now feels that some attempt should be made to contact you (God) or proper authorities."

"Holy, smoking choke cherry bushes! You mean Thistlewaite is going to send God a bill!"

"Mrs. Zofar, please stick to this dictation and all will be made clear. Now to continue—new paragraph.

My client feels that inasmuch as the angelic messenger was apparently off some two thousand years in time, and roughly, some eight or nine thousand miles, geographically, that this matter should be called to your attention."

"Boss, come to think of it, Thistlewaite is a crackpot who is geographically off his nut some nine thousand miles."

"No, Thistlewaite has had a rough time and complaints are in order, I suppose. But the heavenly complaint department closed up a long time ago, I'm afraid."

"Maybe he ought to try the local department store. He does seem to have a new pair of shoes coming. And what *did* happen to his shoes?"

"Funny thing, nobody could find them. But I think they were carried away by the waters in the creek or sunk in the mud some-place. Well, new paragraph.

My client, it must be emphasized, seeks no monetary restitu-tion of the loss of his winter wheat crop, his shoes, subsequent medical bills, or the mental distress undergone by both his wife and himself, for he now feels that this visitation from the angel or 'voice' was much in the same category as the trials and afflictions put upon Job, and that he accepts it as such; however, he strongly feels that the matter of messenger inefficiency should be broached at this time if, for no other reason, than to save others bearing Biblical given or surnames, the pain, shock, and embar-rassment involved in heavenly communication."

"Now boss, please, let's knock this off. I mean come clean. I . . . I . . . can't be a party to this. How can I hold my head up at the monthly meeting of my secretarial group? I mean . . . well, you know."

"Well, I did talk to old Tom Eliphaz on the phone. He's on the neighboring farm. Sold the land to Thistlewaite. He feels, possi-bly, that Thistlewaite was standing near a bush or tree when it was hit by lightning. Eliphaz volunteered the information that Thistlewaite was a crackpot from the word go, anyhow, and still owes for some of his land, and that a lightning bolt was just what he deserved."

"Now this is more like it! Simply have old Cockleburr take out lightning insurance and forget the whole thing."

"Well, he does have health, accident, fire and disaster insurance and all that. But he insists upon my writing this letter, too. A security complex, maybe."

"Why doesn't the local minister say a prayer? Or maybe his psychiatrist could...."

"Mrs. Zofar, we've been asked by his psychiatrist to write this letter as therapy treatment. So, we are back where we started."

"Well, we're at the end of this letter, at least."

"And now, Mrs. Zofar, put on the usual closing."

"Mr. B. There is no *usual* closing in a letter like this."

"Well, ah...I mean, most sincerely yours. No! Your most humble servant, Robert L. Bildad, attorney at law, 821 Symes Building, and so forth."

"Anything else?"

"You know, I've been thinking. I wish I had the nerve to add a postscript. You know, I rather like old Thistlewaite. After all, this is some sort of prayer to his God—a very personal God. A twisted, 20th century prayer—but still a prayer of some kind. Maybe we need more people like Moses J. around."

"Any P.S. then?"

"No, I guess not."

"And one more thing, Mr. B. Do you want I should put a stamp on the envelope? Air mail, maybe?"

KLITZEE ONE—GOD ZERO

Klitzee, how did we call him? Dutch name. I've almost forgotten. Saw it spelled out in the Obit columns. Think it had an exra *a* or *ae* in it. Kalaetzee, maybe. Something like that. We called him Klit or Klitzee. But he's dead now. Dead for a snowflake dead. Maybe we learn something from the Klitzee's of this world? You tell me.

But I was the one who started this snowball rolling, in a way. But then I can't be held responsible. No, I can't. Well, I'm not quite sure. This piece should clear me with Go...oops! The *Administration* as Klitzee would have put it.

Why did I start to say God? That was the exact trouble with old, lank Ichabod-Crane Klitzee: some God-trouble. Some freaks got it bad. A bachelor. Lived with his old mother. He must have been 40 or so. Guess I'll get married when I can. Not brood about it like Klitzee did. Maybe he was a hard-core masturbator. My dad once said all such types come to a bad end. Everybody's dad says this.

But then one November day: "Klitzee," I said. "You're not doing nothing. Come with me to look for a job."

Long, mournful stare from Klitzee. Did he have any other kind? No, come to think on it. A face well-suited to tragedy. Tailor-made by God and company for a bum life-rap. Along with God, Klitzee wanted to believe in girls, too, but didn't. Spent his time reading, as near as I can tell. Jacking-off. Going to endless movies. Playing tennis. That's how we met. He had a good forehand. Always available, so we had a slight, tennis-playing buddyship.

Sundays during bad weather, Klitzee shopped for a religion. Like a consumer dogged by Ralph Nader. You know, was this religion good stuff? Would it stand up under stress? Was some Madison Avenue advertising man lying about it all? He tracked it down like some bloodhound. He looked a bit like a bloodhound around the mouth, but half-starved. Kind of cadaverous, chop-fallen.

"It'll be cold going up in the mountains. You have a good car heater?"

"Not much of one," I said. "Bring a blanket, wrap up your

tootsies."

"You'll never get the lousy job. Born loser like at tennis. Waste the gas."

"So?" I said. That was Klitzee's ending to about every state-ment: *so?* He said, so? to God, I guess. To religion. "So you want me to believe in your God," he said once to one of those earnest Fundamentalist preachers that drift through our town. "So then what? What's the pay-off?" Klitzee walked out in the middle of the minister's long, boring harangue about pay-offs: a comfort-able spot in the cemetery, to hear Klitzee tell about it.

"I'm paying for the gas," I said. "And if you don't eat so damn much, I'll buy our lunch once we get over the pass. What'll you miss around this town for one day? A bum picture show? A book about Bahai? Too wet to play tennis."

"Why do you ask me? Ask one of your slut girl friends."

"No good heater in my car. Only you will go, and we'll talk about God and things."

"Crap!" Klitzee said. But he went with me because I drove by his house and honked the horn. Spur of the moment stuff with Klitzee, like his tennis game. Whammo! Hit for the corners.

The job, a teaching job deep in the Colorado mountains, prom-ised to be a pretty good one as I ski quite a bit, mainly to watch the ski bunnies who drift in from L.A. When the weather's a bit warm they ski topless to drive you crazy. On top of that I needed money bad, and this place was at a small high school where the pay was pretty good all things considered. But Klitzee and I had to drive over a 12,000-foot pass. Icy in spots, but I had thick snow tires, front and rear.

Just before we started over the mountain, Klitzee opened the window to push down the radio aerial. One of the qualifications of Klitzee's coming with me was: "want no damn music, if I go."

"Okay, no sweat," I said. "No reception much in the moun-tains, anyway."

But Klitzee was taking no chances. He rolled the window down to push the antenna deep into its socket. The window wouldn't roll back then. An old car and cranky in all its parts.

"You think I'm gonna drive over the pass with the God-damn window open! You lemme out, here and now!"

"Klitzee! You're always griping!" I got out and tugged and pulled, but the window stuck tight. Apparently, Klitzee, in his frenzy, had stripped the crank rachet. Luckily, I had some old rug samples and a blanket in the back end; I'm the eternal optimist about girls. We stuffed the blanket and the rug in the window space and Klitzee was then obliged to hold them there by leaning his head against the wad.

"Good boy, Klitzee," I said. "That oughta do it!"

"Fat, screwing, fat-head fate!"

To keep Klitzee's mind off our bad luck, I thought I'd better start talking about something. "Funny thing about fat-head fate," I said. "You remember just last year, right around here someplace, those people parked their car by the stream. Why? To eat? Bathe their footies in the creek?"

"I know! I read all about it!" Klitzee came on strong. "Down came a ten-ton boulder. Maybe twenty tons. Crushed them all. The whole blasted family. Blotto! And why? Why!" All this in a rush. I'd hit upon his favorite newspaper-reading matter.

"Why? Wilder's book. *Bridge of San Luis Rey*, that's why."

"You like books. Why'n you try to write?" Klitzee asked then. "You even look like a writer—second-rate. Why'n you write, 'The Friggin Boulder of the Never-Summer Mountains'?"

"But there was another one just like that," I said, warming up to the subject. "Two girls out here from Kansas for a vacation. Stopped by the road in San Juans someplace. For what? Look at the bloody scenery? Down came Mr. Rock. Fifty tons or so. Squashed them both along with their car. Did they look up? Hear anything? A boulder ain't cotton. Makes a big noise as a rule. Nobody the hell knows. Rangers found them both squashed."

"How do you like your two squashed girls, Mr. Death," Klitzee said. And so Klitzee and I talked on about death and fate and he held the rug and blanket over the empty window well and we didn't quite freeze. Talk about fate and death made Klitzee warm and morbidly happy anyway. We got over the pass all right. Very slippery in spots, but the tires held pretty well climbing up.

I had my job interview, and meanwhile Klitzee walked around town, called Frisco. It had one eating place open. A Cow Queen drive-in for God's sake. Not up to Klitzee's high standards.

"Nothing much to my life but good food," he once said to me. So he was fussy, and mad that he'd come along on this job trip with me. "Dirty hamburger full of grease," he said afterwards when I picked him up following my interview. "Luke warm coffee. I shoulda committed *hari-kari* right on their dirty doorstep. A monument in stone should be erected on the spot: 'Klitzee Ate Here. Died in Agony'!"

"Cool it. You're turning my stomach. When we get back over the pass, I'll buy you another sandwich."

Serve the bastards right if I'd thrown up against their show window. Dirty little red-head waitress, too, No ring on her grimy hand, but with a kid. Hers. Dirty red-haired brat with his nose drooling, running around the place, bothering the customers. Life is all-around dirty."

"Yeah," I said. "I'll buy that, I guess. Don't think I'll get this teaching job. They demanded a wrestling coach to boot, plus teaching five straight courses in botany. Then on weekends I'd have to go on the road over the passes with a sweaty wrestling team. Turn the bus over the hill. Get fired."

"Get dead, most likely," Klitzee said.

We started back over the pass. Both of us disappointed: Klitzee with food, me with the idea I'd have to coach wrestling rather than skiing. Not much point being in ski land U.S.A. unless you could ski on weekends. It was sunset when we started back; a wind chill about 50 below, I'd say. Klitzee held grimly to his blanket and rug, but the air swept in. He looked blue, more cadaverous by the minute. Why did I bring him?

So, I hurried back home. Once over the pass there was a half-way decent place to get some booze, a warm fire. The west side of the mountain was pretty good. The highway crew had put some sand on the curves. But not so on the east side. I figured we had these big snow tires and all would be well. But I hit one curve just past the summit too fast. We were just past the top of the crest, high. I mean, a good 11,000-feet altitude. It was some 1,000 feet or so straight down the cliff side. And no guard rails. We all live dangerously in Colorado. Like to scare the crap out of the touristas, maybe? So they won't come back? Place too crowded already? Who knows? But we don't have much tax money for super-safe, four-lane highways on the 12,000-foot passes.

So as I say, I hit the curve too fast. Nobody around luckily; I mean, nobody coming up the other way on this narrow two-laner. In a second, we went into a beauty fast figure-eight skid. We whirled around out of control much like on a snap-the-whip ride in an amusement park.

Klitzee, the doom-like man, grabbed my arm. I think I glanced briefly into his eyes: they burned with holy fire. "This is it! This is it!" he yelled.

Myself, I was going to jump out, but Klitzee had my arm and he had a blanket wrapped around his head and one over his knees. He wouldn't have made it. I felt, I suppose, (although there wasn't much time for reflection), that it was my duty as captain of this skidding monster to go down with my ship, sort of. But maybe not. If Klitzee hadn't had my arm in a death grip, I probably would have skipped out my door into a snow bank. Don't know, exactly.

But to continue: we skidded backwards toward the edge of the road and the cliff. Fast, I mean. I was certain we'd plunge on over, guard rails or no guard rails. The cliff was almost straight down. I'd say an 85 percent grade. Maybe the snow would stop us. We were too high up for the pine trees to brake our fall. Don't really know what might have happened to us, heading for eternity backwards over the god-damn cliff. But I will say if you're going to die in a plunge it must be one hundred times better to die head first.

But we stopped. My heavy Scout car slid to a halt. There was a gentle bump. We hit, I'd say, a six-inch barrier of snow that the highway crew accidentally had piled up along the edge of the road. Not enough, it seemed to me, to stop a 4,000-pound car from going on over. But we stopped.

Both Klitzee and myself, white and shaken.

"I'm a son-of-a-bitch, we ain't dead!" Klitzee managed to say. He said this over and over, too, as we drove slowly down the pass. In the next town we stopped at a bar. Got a drink. Klitzee insisted upon paying for the booze. "What good would money have been up there," he said.

I bought the next drink, however. Klitzee was silent for a long time as we stared into the fireplace. Then: "How come we stopped? Couldn't happen again. Shall I say in a million years?"

"Two million," I said. Don't know why I blurted out my next statement. Wrong guy to say it to. Agnostic, atheist Klitzee, the great religious shopper: "Boy," I wheezed after my second double-bourbon, "that was the hand of God! Raised right up and pushed our car back on the road. No other explanation."

"Bull shit," Klitzee said. "Must have been a stone guard rail under that little hunk of snow."

"Don't think so," I said.

"I'll find out," Klitzee came back. And he said something typical next. At the time I didn't think much of it. "If that son-of-a-bitch creep put up his hand to stop us, I owe him something. Can't be in debt to a no-good like god . . . or fate, whoever he is. What did I ever do for him? Zero!"

"Well, it was me, Klitzee. Luckily you were riding with me, that's all. He wasn't gonna kill a good ski coach and botany high school teacher like I'm. Gotta suffer some more before he pushes me over a cliff. That's his bag, you know. Kick the jerks around a bit until they're punchy—and then, whammo!"

Klitzee didn't say a lot after my outburst. Muttered in his drink. I didn't listen too closely. The bar maid had on a super mini-skirt.

I dropped Klitzee from my small roster of friends, at least pretty much, after this near-accident thing. I guess I was embarrassed at my punk mountain driving. Me, a skier! Been over all the winter passes in the state; never skidded out of control before. Klitzee was a Jonah-type, that was all. A morbid drudge, a mommy-sponger. Didn't want him around, really. But I did take him out for a beer after what proved to be our last tennis game.

But later, after he went on the carbon-monoxide trip with a car—a *borrowed* car, mind you! I started on this Thornton Wilder, *Bridge of San Luis Rey* stuff on him. Pieced it together. Seems he borrowed a car the very next week after our skid. Went back. Looked at the tiny ridge that had stopped our car. Kicked it with his foot. Not satisfied. Looked down over the edge. Almost straight down (checked on this, too, after the suicide). No trees for a good 200 yards down. Nothing to stop our car, but maybe deep snow. But would our heavy Scout have skidded down. Started an avalanche? Buried us? Who knows? Even I, a guy who lives for today mainly, gave a thought to why no cars were coming up the other way. We would have banged into them unmercifully and knocked them over the road.

After our last tennis game, and when I took him out for this beer, Klitzee had grabbed me by the sweat shirt. Pulled me close. He had bad breath, I remember. "Why the hell are we here drinking this drink. Not dead over the pass?"

"Bosh!" I came back. "You still on this kick?" I was still feeling a bit guilty about it all. "We would have just slid down the mountain, easy like. Nothing drastic. Might have had a hard time climbing back up to the road for help though. Could have froze to death. The wind chill must have been around 60 below, I figure. But anyway, here we are in this dandy bar today. Drinking this delicious, character-building beer and we..."

"No sense to it! No sense to it at all," he said. His dark brooding eyes seemed to kindle. I remember too his big nose, hooked like Thoreau's. His bad breath.

"Better not think about it anymore," I said.

"Ka-rappe!" Klitzee said. "That was Hemingway's remedy for everything in the fate line. *Better not think about it.* Big deal! He's the guy that shot himself! The irony of it all! Better not think about it!" Klitzee began to mock my tone of voice in a high-pitched wheeze. "It's man's duty to think about just that! Nothing else. Not dames, not jobs..." And then in mid-speech he looked at me and stopped. Very likely my trivial, shallow, shoe-button eyes weren't vibing with his vibes. It was the beer, maybe. Too bad.

As I say, after this last time at a bar, I dropped Klitzee flat. Too morbid. The compleat bore. I remember how, earlier in our friendship, I tried to get him fixed up once. What a frost that was! He talked Spengler to this little chicklet I had him lined up with. Spengler, for cripe's sake! I was in the front seat of the car, making out. And Klitzee was in the back seat talking about Spengler. His girl never heard of old Oscar and would have loved to talk maybe something about contraceptives? In fact, I heard her ask him: "What do you think about the pill?"

What a lead-in for a quick back-seat make! But old Klitzee went blank. "What pill?" he asked.

The girl in question never went with me after that. Called me up, too, for a semi-obscene phone call and said: "Blind date! Bug off, fatso!" Slammed the phone. And there went one of my lays. Not too many around either when you're an unemployed school teacher. So, I felt Klitzee was a bad-luck charm. Put the kibosh on any fun thing—thinking about God. Worse still, talking it all to death.

He phoned me once, too, just before the monoxide thing. "I want to go back."

Playing dumb to get rid of the creep, I said: "Hey! Klitzee! That's a title of a song: 'I wanna go back to my lil' grass shack in coca-cola Hawaii or something'."

"Drive me back to the pass," Klitzee went on in his flat voice.

"Hell no," I said. "Rent a car, Klitzee. I'm busy."

Well, it seems he did go back. Twice more. Hired, get this, a civil engineer, a guy experienced in building roads. They went up there. The engineer said the wrong thing, no doubt about it. Klitzee had marked the curve in his mind and put some kind of rock cairn near the spot. I can see it all in my mind. The engineer got out of Klitzee's rented car. Nervous like. Afraid of the traffic that whizzed by them on the narrow road. Wondering if this kook Klitzee would ever pay him for his trouble. Kicked at the little snow barrier with his foot. Asked: "How much did the Scout car weigh? Three thousand pounds or so?" Then the road expert said the wrong thing: "You had God on your side, Mister, that's all."

Wrong thing to say to a non-god man. Klitzee didn't much want God on his side. Just science and engineering. That's all. A stubborn Dutchman.

Klitzee left a note for his poor old mother: *To whom it may concern—No choice about my entrance. But I have the last word about the exit.* And then like a postscript: *I'll be damned if I'll be beholden to that...that . . .* And then an ink smudge. Then another note, clipped to this: *Anyway, we're all going to die slowly of monoxide in this Polluted World—why not speed it up?*

His mother showed me the note for as she put it, I was his "close friend."

Guess I was among the few who knew what Klitzee meant. Maybe not. Klitzees are the kind that make you unsure of anything. Went to his funeral. Not many others there. His mother and I guess his insurance man. The civil engineer, maybe? A tennis player or two? My current chick went with me. I conned her into going. We stood in the snow, coming down hard. Heard the minister mention God as they lowered his coffin. Was about to step up and say: "Jesus, man! Cool it! Klitzee wouldn't want that old malarkey!" But too late. Too shy with his old mother there.

My kitten looked up at me then with a what-a-hell-of-a-place-to-bring-a-date look. "A *Funeral* for crumb's sake!" she hissed in my ear as we tramped in the snow back to our car.

"Better not think about it," was all I could say in reply.

THE RABBIT THAT LOST ITS NOSE

There was Barney, the brown-nosed rabbit, and then there was the machine, the mechanism. Trim, efficient, smug, the machine with its slatted, eye-like vents for sucking in air, held Phocian's attention as he worked stacking the neat cylinders, checking the valves. It gave Phocian some vague sort of comfort to let his eyes wander first to the machine, and then to Barney. Barney was there just in case the machine became confused; Barney, with his high metabolic rate, his rapid heart beat, was not apt to be confused. He would merely die. The machine, when it sucked in an incorrect sample of oxygen, would not die, but simply sound its terrible, terrible claxon cry: a sound not too unlike Phocian's own private world. True, Phocian had heard the sound only once or twice, but it was an ugly sound, a twentieth-century sound that cut through the world's nonsense: "the dance-is-over" sound. And Phocian never forgot it.

Despite the claxon and its meaning, Phocian was not too unhappy working in the arsenal—an arsenal that manufactured nerve gas in some unthinking, mindless sort of way. It made Phocian feel more vital, more alive to be so close to instant death. Perhaps, he thought, he received as a fringe benefit the same alert, tingling sensation a snake charmer must feel working with his basket of writhing cobras. It, the nerve gas, was not unlike the bite of a cobra. When the gas, odorless, colorless, sometimes leaked out of the cylinder containers, its effect was very much like the sting of a serpent, and the saying was around the plant that so-and-so "got bit" last month or last year. The gas attacked the nerve centers; one died of a paralyzed diaphragm.

To be sure, all kinds of precautions were taken at the arsenal so there would be precious few of the "bites"—but when one works in a flour mill, one gets flour on the clothes. The men in the cylinder division wore gas masks most of the time, and sometimes clumsy, uncomfortable rubber suits, for it was dangerous to wear wool or any fabric the gas could cling to. Phocian had been present at an "accident" only one time when Buff, the colored janitor, had stacked a few gas cylinders out of the way to make room for his sweeping. It was after hours and Buff had thus been careless about regulations and had neglected to wear his rubber suit.

In touching a tank, he somehow had jostled a valve, and the gas, in its insidious way, had nestled in Buff's wool sweater. Later on, pulling the sweater over his head in the plant locker room, Buff suddenly had dropped unconscious to the floor. There had not been enough gas to set off the warning claxon, or alarm Barney, but just enough to "bite" Buff. They worked on him: Ralph, the foreman, and Phocian. Ralph had quickly opened Buff's eyelids to see if the pupils were pinpointed, then started artificial respiration.

They took turns working on Buff as a drowned person, keeping him alive until the doctor arrived and performed a tracheotomy, and brought him back to the world, but it had been a narrow squeak.

When Phocian told his wife, Fanny, about the mishap (it had been kept out of the papers), she begged him once again to quit. She wrinkled up her forehead, and clutched one of her long, blonde-gray pigtails. "It all makes me feel like a wife of a jet pilot. I don't know if you're ever coming home for dinner."

Phocian had laughed and patted her on the bum. "But think of the extra money, honey. And the insurance. You get a clean $20,000 if I get a whiff of that gas—some punkins, eh? You can buy a fresh, clean boyfriend, a Caddy or two, and start life all over."

"You like danger, uh?" his wife asked. "Great for me and the kids, not knowing if you'll come home on a slab blue and dead— dead for what? A few extra bucks a month?"

"Dead for a ducat dead," Phocian had said then.

"And you can can that Shakespeare jazz any time now," Fanny said, squinting her eyes, holding tight to one pigtail. "I used to think it was great you quoting Shakespeare and...and...the rest of them, but now..."

"Now what?"

"I'll take a milkman who quotes baseball scores and who comes home at night in one piece."

"I've heard dangerous stories about milkmen, too," Phocian came back, and that ended the argument for the time being.

But no, it was not that: not the danger, not the money that kept Phocian on the job. What was it then? Sometimes he would ask Barney when he and Barney were all alone in the storage room, for to Phocian had fallen the job of last check up before the arsenal shut down each day. "Barney," Phocian would say, pressing his nose against the big cage that Barney shared with three other male rabbits, "why are we here?" Or was it Barney that asked the question? At times, Phocian wasn't quite sure.

Barney was a huge Belgian rabbit with an absurd brown-tipped nose that gave him a peculiar, clown-like expression. Barney was friendly, especially to Phocian who usually carried lettuce or carrots in his lunch box, feeding Barney and the others faithfully. Barney would hop over to the bars when Phocian appeared, his brown, clown-like nose twitching, his lustrous, pink-rimmed eyes looking trustingly at Phocian. "Barney, why are we here?" Barney had no answer but to approach the cage bars, his eyes full of love for Phocian.

Often, in the dim light of the cylinder room, Barney's brown-tip nose gave the impression that some of it—the vital part—was missing, for the rest of Barney was snowy white, and it appeared that the nose somehow stopped short of being a true nose. This illusion gave Phocian an uneasy feeling. "Barney, we need that nose of yours in here. We can't, indeed, have a comic nose, a false, artificial nose that won't tell us true." Then Phocian would feed Barney a carrot and reach out suddenly to touch Barney's nose to see if it was really there, and Barney would ease back out of reach, but rescuing the carrot in his mouth, unscathed by Phocian's touch.

Most of the time, however, it was fairly clear to Phocian why he was at the gas arsenal: because it was so pointless, so useless. The time, he remembered when he had wanted to be a poet, at a tender age it was, something like the boy Rolvaag. Like the Norwegian writer, Phocian had spoken up to his father bravely. "I want to be a poet." But Phocian's father had answered back: "But that's so useless in this day and age!" And failing, quickly, as a poet perhaps Phocian deliberately sought for a pointless occupation, for he had felt duty bound to oppose his father.

Phocian reflected that it was not the extra money, not the danger entirely. It was the utter absurdity that attracted him to the job. Like poetry, he reasoned, the job was a charming anachronism. The gas was first mixed and blended in huge metal tanks, special lead containers; then it was sifted down, blown through pipes to smaller containers where new substances were added, and finally it was piped into small, neat cylinders of an ideal size to be carried by planes and dropped or sprayed on an enemy. These cylinders were then shipped to so-called "strategic areas" of the country to be again stored in larger warehouses— very likely stored forever, as old poems are filed away, for the gas was no longer an efficient war weapon, as poems, Phocian felt, were no longer capable of arousing men's passions.

There wasn't any good purpose for the military to insist on its manufacture, for the gas was outdated, useless and dangerous to have around—very much like poetry. But perhaps it was good for psychological reasons: like piling up gold in Ft. Knox; it gave the country a vague sense of security. All this Phocian explained to Barney after hours as Barney stoically munched on a lettuce leaf. "I'm really a teller of fairy tales," Phocian said to Barney. "I frighten little children into being good."

But then, on practical days, Phocian would tell Barney: "The reason we are here, you goofy rabbit, is strictly money. Not so much money for me and carrots for you, but money for the big boys." Then Phocian would wink, confidentially, as if he were privy to top state secrets. Barney's comic brown nose would twitch at this, and Phocian would whisper, "You silly beast! I mean the chemical lobby at work in Washington!"

It was this aspect, too, that Phocian liked: the mindlessness of it all. The country, the military, kept piling up these endless cylinders of gas, which were dangerous and a nuisance to store, which were deucedly awkward to get rid of or destroy should the war danger suddenly be over with. In truth, it was a wonderful, absurd occupation, and at times Phocian felt some pleasure at being connected with it.

"We could build...ah...bowling alleys, make bubble gum, hospitals, free carrots for rabbits, anything! Eh, Barney? But no, we make deadly gas. And this is wonderful in a queer sort of way. Don't you see, you fathead rabbit? We got a real nutty world cooking here—after God's own black heart."

So Phocian's life went on in working, and in conversations with Barney, and in less pertinent conversations with Fanny.

Fanny, unlike Barney, would not twitch her nose, but twitch

her fanny in a semi-seductive way and demand answers on practical things. But there was nothing to tell her; he was much in the
position of Barney in this respect. Sometimes it seemed to Phocian that it was not so much a matter of defending his reason for
having such a job, but defending his marriage, which, too, was
rather absurd on the face of it.

He often wanted to ask Fanny, "Why are we here in this odd
domestic setup?" But Fanny's behind would twitch when he got
too philosophical and they would end up in bed, threshing
mindlessly, madly, between the sheets. There was, indeed, some
answer in this, but Phocian didn't quite know what it was.

Domestic affairs with him were a problem, and like the job
resisted easy answers. Phocian had always been a restless, rootless person, shifting from place to place. He had been a
millwright as a young man, but this had gone out of style as
millwrights were obsolete. Then Fanny had prevailed upon him
to take a civil service exam, listing his millwright experience, and
the government eventually decided he would be an excellent
plant maintenance man in the gas arsenal: a man to check on the
cylinders to see if the gas was blowing correctly from the large
tanks to the small ones, if the valves were set tightly, and if the
containers were trustworthy.

As for his marriage: this had been restless, rootless, too. He
had met Fanny in a huge rabbit warren—Levittown. They had
both been something like Barney, sniffing at the bars of their
cages, asking questions as to the why and how. Fanny had been
married to a milkman; he was never home in the mornings,
which was perhaps the downfall of everything, or perhaps the
beginning. Phocian had an evening job, and was home alone in
the mornings. His wife, Lisa, had worked as a school teacher.
They had no children, but Fanny had one, Marcy. Then the Levittown sections were always throwing parties; Phocian found it
was easy to drift into these "block parties" which sometimes
turned into casual key-parties, or, to be more accurate, wife-
trading parties.

Not that Fanny or Phocian had ever gone quite this far. Fanny
had refused to toss her key in the pile. Or, if she had, Phocian was
so drunk that one night he was a little vague about events, but he
was pretty sure Fanny had kept her door double-bolted, so there

was no hanky-panky then. Of Lisa's perambulations, he wasn't so sure.

Then, he had taken to going over to Fanny's in the morning to drink coffee and to complain about his job, his hangover, or Lisa. They had gotten to talking, and he to quoting Shakespeare, and one thing led to another. Here again there had been no final answers as to why he, Phocian, was in the brown house with the green porch, and she, Fanny, was some thirty yards away in a green house with a brown porch. And so to defy God, and his whimsical, mindless ways, they one day traded spouses. Quickly and neatly one morning, Fanny had packed her grips, taken Marcy, and left her husband, Frank. Her farewell note read, "Stew's on the stove and drop dead!" Phocian had merely locked the doors and left Lisa a note: "I've lost my mind."

And they had flown to Denver and the West and here they were, not in a rabbit-hutch housing project this time, but still rootless, unsettled, casual; and the basic questions went unanswered. They had actually married at the grave risk of bigamy charges, although they both had written several letters back to Levittown and had both received no answers. But Fanny did have much prettier eyes, deeper eyes than Lisa, and she did have a child, proof that she was, in the right sense, creative, and this seemed to give some reason for his move. And now they had a child of their own, Robert, age two, and life seemed to have more meaning to Phocian than before.

But really this, too, was absurd. If his first wife, Lisa, had been fruitful, and he had not lived in Levittown with its green porches and brown-painted roofs, or green roofs and brown porches, would all this have happened?

—*But it is not good to question everything, everything.*

Phocian had been taught this last statement about questions in a dream. Phocian dreamed much more now that he was working in a gas arsenal. The dreams were not about twitching female behinds so much as about rabbits; mostly about Barney, the brown-nosed rabbit. Often he saw Barney in his dreams, hopping down a long, long hall. And he did have to admit that Barney's white flag of a tail looked somewhat attractive. So perhaps his dreams were still a bit Freudian, but not as much as when he had been living with Lisa in Levittown. Lisa's fanny didn't twitch at all, but was like some wax-white, flaccid hunk of lard, a lump of dough to be kneaded to his desires... hardly dream-provoking.

But there, anyway, was Barney in his dreams now, hopping down the long hallway. "Remember!" Barney says to Phocian in the dream, the oft-repeated dream, "Think not!" And then Barney disappears down a hole, much like the white rabbit in *Alice in Wonderland*.

"But your nose is gone," Phocian shouts after him in the dream, "and you have no watch! You *must* look at your watch!" Phocian shouts down the black hole Barney has scampered into, "for time is running out for both of us!" But there is no answer, except a vague sound from the tunnel which Phocian feels must be the phrase, "Think not! The eleventh commandment!" "But... but," Phocian stammers down the hole: "You have been reading *Moby Dick*! And rabbits don't read Melville!"

And then Phocian always wakes up at this point, screaming aloud, "Rabbits don't read Melville!" over and over, and his wife shakes him and sometimes asks, "What about Melville?" And Phocian answers sleepily, "He's my boss down at the plant." And Fanny rolls over, twitching her behind, and goes fast asleep, and Phocian gets up to go to his job and Barney, not knowing quite which is the dream, and which is not.

Since the accident to Buff, the job, for Phocian, has taken on more of a dream-like quality. And once when the claxon horn sounded by mistake (Barney, Phocian said proudly at the time, never makes a mistake), and Phocian heard again that horrible, unearthly noise, and saw his colleagues stumbling around with their gargoyle-like gas masks on, he could not eat his lunch that day, and he walked the sandy, drear wastes outside the arsenal (for the plant was put far away from human kind), and walking in the desert, Phocian took the clarion call of the claxon as some personal summons to justify his life, to ask himself, once again, "What am I really doing here in this time and this place?"

Of course, there was no answer, only sand and dust blowing in his face, and so that same night with the soft bedroom lights on, he said aloud to his new-found god, The Claxon Horn, whose voice was the voice of Hell Made Real, "It is my hatred for humanity. It's nice to be busy at work, work like some malicious Machiavellian ant, piling up death and misery for human kind. That's why I'm here!"

But this tack didn't quite satisfy him, and as he drifted off to sleep, he said quietly in Fanny's ear, "I'm really mad at God. Yes! I have the impertinence to be angry. Mad at him for not giving reason or meaning to this life; that a job as a milkman or a poison gas manufacturer makes no damn difference!" Fortunately for domestic tranquility, Fanny was fast asleep.

Phocian stared then at his sleeping wife. If only he had been a poet, he would write a complaint to God that he, Phocian, was owed the dignity of being consulted before being set adrift on this raft, on this outrageous sea, to battle against what? Himself mostly? Maybe making gas to kill people somehow evened the score against God ... gave purpose to his own, lone life? But then there was Barney the rabbit, and Fanny, and Marcy, and now little Robert. What had they to do with it? In truth, Barney especially had begun to get under his skin; his life depended upon Barney: machines were not to be trusted. A Barney sniffing the gas in time, Barney's pupils turning small, Barney rolling over stiff and dead—these were the things to give shape and substance to this world. Phocian told himself, over and over like a nun telling her beads, *Barney has a higher metabolic rate, his heart beats faster and he can detect odorless, mindless gas* THAT SEEPS THROUGH THE WHOLE WORLD STRIKING DOWN ITS CREATOR, MAN, IN A MINDLESS WAY, UNTHINKING, UNMEANING, UNCARING, UNLOVING AND LOVING BOTH.

It was true that Barney can detect the gas before the machine, before I, Phocian, can, and does this not mean, then, Phocian thought, that animals are superior to men? They can detect harm ahead of man, for did not the deer sense trouble, the rabbits streak away, before man and his gun stabbed their horizon? And was this not a world of guns?

It was after one of his dreams of Barney: Barney had seemed so real the night in question, and he had caught Barney this time before he could dart down his tunnel, and in this twilight world he stroked the soft fur, and felt for his funny brown nose that wasn't there, and he had awakened then, his hands on Fanny's pure white breasts. And she had rolled over and had said, "For God's sake, it's only six in the morning and it's time for your breakfast, and it's go-to-work time, not go-to-bed-and-grunt time!"

"You're so damn delicate about our sex life," Phocian had said in reply. And then Phocian had gotten up. But he remembered then that Barney had said something to him in the dream. "Think not," Barney had said again, and Phocian had caught him and, in the dream, had asked, "Why? Why think not?" And Barney had answered him something, oh, so wise, and so true! But Fanny's restlessness with his hands on her breasts had broken off the dream, and so it, what the rabbit had said, was gone now.

Phocian stumbled around the kitchen, getting his own breakfast and packing his lunch. He put in three carrots this time, for Barney, and he wondered why. And he thought even then, at seven in the morning, *this will be the last time—I won't have to go through this again! . . . the temptations of the flesh, and the food for Barney, and the going to work and the making of the deadly gas, and not hearing the answer to the vital questions.* But then he didn't know for sure, and he shrugged off this feeling. But at five o'clock when the quitting bell rang, Phocian knew that this was the last day: there was no sense going on, threshing on the bed with Fanny, feeding Barney, piling up cylinder after cylinder of poison gas.

At six p.m. Buff came around checking on things and Phocian was still there wondering how to go about the deed.

"Working late tonight?" Buff asked.

"Poison, poison everywhere, and not a drop to drink," Phocian answered.

"What's that you say, white boy?"

"I wonder if you could do me a favor? Can you drive to town for me and get coffee and sandwiches?" Phocian proffered a bill.

"Well, I have my sweeping to do, boss. Ain't this pretty unusual—you staying late this way? I mean, real late?"

"Just this once, Buff, and you can keep the change." It was a big bill and Buff hesitated, but not for long. "Here are the keys to my car," Phocian said, and then, in a minute, Buff was gone.

When Buff shut the door, a big, clanging, air-tight metal door, Phocian went quickly to the large cage. Shoving Barney unceremoniously aside, Phocian grabbed the other two rabbits by the ears and tossed them out the metal door into the desert waste. "Godspeed," he said. Then he took a cylinder of gas and climbed into the cage with Barney. "I have something here, Barney, that you will be interested in." Barney approached cautiously, hoping for a carrot.

"This is the gas, Barney, that was to prove to the world the Nazis were the master race." Barney, unimpressed, hopped to the far end of the cage. "I will turn this valve, Barney, and our pupils will pinpoint and our breathing will subside, and then...and then...this will prove to the world that...that... well, nothing."

Barney's comic nose twitched at this and his eyes looked at Phocian half with love, half with fear. "But Barney," Phocian said in half-hearted tones, "one of us has to play God.'" But then, suddenly, Phocian knew that his statement had been more of a question than an answer. And the wise thing that Barney had said to him in the last dream? Perhaps, Phocian thought, it is better not to have a nose in a world of evil smells. Just smile sweetly, Barney had said, and hope for a carrot instead of Buchenwald, and all will be well in time.

Clutching Barney to his chest, scrambling out of the cage, Phocian then took the gas cylinder, turned the valve and dashed it to the floor, shutting the huge metal door behind him. Safe outside, they both listened for the claxon's mournful sound, and, in a minute, the arsenal was full of armed guards.

"What the hell is going on here!" a watchman yelled.

"The...the sensor machine. I was just testing," Phocian yelled above the horn.

"We had no damn orders on an air test," a guard said. "I'll have to report this."

"Yes, I know," Phocian said.

"We'll have to get the decontamination squad in there. This all costs money."

"Yes, I know," said Phocian. "But it's worth it."

For his unauthorized testing of the air sensor, Phocian was summarily discharged. Somehow he managed to talk his superior into letting him keep Barney. "For a souvenir of a mis-spent life," Phocian explained.

"Well, I'll have to take him and them other two males out of your last pay check—plus the decontamination squad costs. You'll have about enough money left for two beers."

"One for you and one for me, okay? And then Godspeed."

That same evening, as Fanny met him at the door, Phocian

announced that he had been fired. "All I have to show for it is this one rabbit I brought home for little Marcy."

"Thank God!" Fanny said. "I'll go fix some rabbit stew and Marcy can learn to play with her head or something."

"Not this rabbit. He's had a bit of the gas. Ruins the meat forever."

Jobless, Phocian sat around the house for two weeks, feeding Barney, playing with Marcy and Robert. Marcy had been overjoyed with Barney. "But it looks like his nose is missing," she said.

"Never you mind," Phocian answered. "He don't need a nose around here."

One day Phocian said to Fanny: "Hell, you know? I don't think I'll ever go back to working."

"It just so happens," Fanny said, "I've about landed you a new job. My milkman, who is getting worried about the milk bill, says..."

"Don't you go getting any ideas about milkmen. Not one of them can quote Shakespeare."

"Creep! I mean my *new* milkman tells me there's a job opening down at his plant."

"Nope. Too hard to jump from poison gas to milk for the kiddies all at once like. Gotta work down easy: machine guns, hunting knives, and then maybe to can openers. Better let me think it over."

"Well, they've got sort of a decontamination machine down there that warns when the fallout gets too high in the milk. Then it washes it out and cleans it up ready for drinking."

"So?"

"So, they need a maintenance man. You'd be ideal."

"How does this machine warn everybody about fallout?"

"How should I know. Rings a damn bell maybe. Blows a claxon horn like at the gas works." Phocian's face fell at this. "But I'm sure they'll let you change it," Fanny said.

"I'd like to hook up the 'Bell Song' from *Lakme*. You know, those beautiful little temple bells that go *tinkle*."

"I'm sure they'll let you hook up temple bells, Phocian baby. They're used to all kinds of kooks in a milk plant."

PHOCIAN

Phocian hadn't been a cow for very damn long when one of those spooky, long-tailed magpies came swooping down into the clover field and started pecking at something in the grass not two feet away. A magpie never would have come so close to a man and it made Phocian feel, at last, a kinship with the world: that he was truly a part of things and not just an observer any more.

Phocian went "moo" with joy and moved ever so little towards the bird. The magpie jumped a few saucy steps, making a sound like "zippa zippa," and eyed Phocian as if to say, "What goes on here? You'n me are buddies, ain't we?" And then it went on pecking at something in the lush green grass of the large meadow. The something it was pecking looked to Phocian like the carcass of a squirrel. Phocian thought then that it was nice to be a cow and that he wouldn't mind it any more when the rain came down.

Phocian's first week as a cow had been the hardest; that is, Phocian had seemed to remember something of his dying and his transmigration. He had hoped he would become at least an eagle and could find shelter in a hole in a cliff, and it was quite a shock to find that he was a cow, forced to stand unprotected in a pasture. One day, in the other life, when he had been quite old and cricked with pain, Phocian remembered that he had been pushed out on the hospital terrace by his nurse. Of a sudden, he'd felt a chill and a strange numbness, and he could no longer move his limbs or head. He could only see straight ahead at a patch of sky through the trees.

Phocian remembered that it had been a fairly cloudy day, and he could see something on the order of a sunset, but then he knew it was far too early in the day for that. He saw this sky, interlaced with darkish, serrated strips of clouds that made a broad, wavering, ladder-effect upwards. Suddenly, Phocian had sensed that this was perhaps his last sight on earth as a man: this sky, with grayish and pink cloud strips and dazzling light beyond. Staring hungrily at his last patch of sky, he knew somehow that he was not going to die, but merely change form. Phocian had felt then, for the first time in his sixty-three years, that he was part of nature, part of that bit of sky, and he had mumbled a small prayer asking that he might return as an eagle to the world.

Then his eyes had begun to fail and he could no longer see the patch of sky, and as his head sank to his chest, he could see only a portion of his hospital blanket; he could see the fine fibers of the blanket, waving like silver grass in a field. And then this, too, had begun to fade and he was aware of much hustling and bustling at his side, and his chair was pushed into the hospital corridor, and someone had forced his head back and his eyes fell upon the clock over the desk of the head nurse. He was having a hard time breathing, watching the second hand of the large clock and trying to breathe each time the hand moved.

And as Phocian lay dying in the hospital corridor, he watched the clock tick, and the second hand go through its measured motions, and then it occurred to Phocian that he was now time itself; he was the clock on the wall, the second hand that went 'tick, tick'. And this was a fine feeling for Phocian, but then, at the same instant, he was the rain drop on the window, the dust molecule in the air, the wind in the branches, a leaf turning pale green in the sun, a blade of grass—he was all this and at once. But Phocian preferred to be the second hand on the clock on the wall, and he gathered all his forces for this, and he stayed on the wall for a long, long time. Tick, tick, tick he went, and the light ebbed and flowed in the hall for he knew not how long, for this was best, Phocian reasoned: to be time itself; a tick in the vast silence, a quick darting movement of a second hand in a nothingness.

Phocian thought soon then that he would go, as time, as a ticking sound, to visit the forehead of a lady he despised, one who had remained forever young, and he would go there as time to her house, and say tick tick to the creases in her skin and they would deepen as if by magic, and she would get older and older by the second—by his second—and there would be enjoyment in that. But Phocian delayed in his plan, and stayed on the clock on the wall in the hospital corridor, for time was more vital where there was much pain.

Once, the electricity went off (for Phocian inhabited an electric clock) and the clock stopped, but Phocian, with a sweet smile, went right on inside of himself: tick, tick, tick. And finally a janitor came and put the clock to rights, but he did not hear

Phocian say in his ariel voice: "This won't help. I'm ten thousand ticks ahead of you."

But after a while, it palled on Phocian to be time, a mere tick on the wall, and with a will he gathered himself up. He went then to the rain drop on the window, the blade of grass nodding in the wind, the wind itself fluttering in the willows, the dust spiraling downwards to a grass carpet in the sunlight. He went to all these things, one by one, and took part of himself from each leaf and tree, holding himself tightly as a newly-gathered bunch of faggots for the fire, and he ran into the woods, carrying himself, and put each part of him down in a corner of a meadow.

"Let us see what we have now," he said to himself. And like a miser he began to count, to create himself from bits of sun and grass and wind and trees. But Phocian found, to his surprise, that in gathering his separate selves, he had forged a cow; that he now was a cow, standing in a field, and he was an entity unto himself. But he felt a strange kinship for all these things he had been, the rain drop, the grass, the wind, and so when the magpie alighted at his feet in the field he felt a strange joy, and he said "moo" again to the magpie to tell him that they all were brothers.

In Phocian's first few weeks as a cow he found that his thoughts were mostly cow-like, and for the most part he had cow-like sensibilities. And yet, those first few weeks there seemed still to be a man-hangover; Phocian could vaguely remember being a man and having man-thoughts. But it did not trouble him too much. It was, after all, nice to be a cow except for the part of being left out in the rain and snow. Then too, 'he' was a 'she' now, but Phocian still regarded himself as a man, or of the male sex, despite his return to earth as a milk cow.

As to the rain, Phocian once had been left out in a hard spring downpour and he had shambled over to the barn, but the gate leading to the barn area had been closed. His owner, a farmer named Willis, had not seemed to care too much about his livestock, and Phocian was quite horrified and restless standing in the mud in a storm. But then he found he didn't feel the rain and wind as intensely as he used to. He had scraped against a barbed wire fence, too, when some other cows had jostled him and the barbs had cut fairly deeply into his foreleg, but he felt little or nothing. He was Mother Nature's child for sure now and she took care of him, that was all. Phocian found that stormy days were best anyway because the people from the farm weren't about: nobody would come out in the rain to bother him except perhaps at milking time. But sunny days were pleasant too.

Luckily, Phocian was a milk cow and thus there was no abbatoir in the offing. Phocian attempted to laugh when he thought of the phrase, "abbatoir in the offing." Farmer Willis' eyes would pop out of his head if he knew that one of his cows was so literate as to make such a statement. Phocian felt vaguely embarrassed that the phrase was a bit on the corny side, but then, as a cow, it was the very best he could think of. Yes, it was lucky he was a milk cow. He didn't mind too much at being milked, either. He had squirmed and switched his tail frantically the first time the hired man had run his cold, rough hands over him, and the whole business had struck him as rather undignified for an ex-man. But later on it gave Phocian great satisfaction to know that he was thereby giving something to the world—and asking for nothing in return, really, but the chance to crop a few blades of grass in the pasture.

Best of all, Phocian liked the birds who trusted him. Some of them, the sparrows, would perch on his shoulders and chirp confidently away about various matters of concern to sparrows. He tried to talk to some of them, but then all words seemed to come out "moo"; even "abbatoir in the offing" came out "moo". But that was all right; the birds didn't seem to care one way or the other. Words were pretty much of a waste of time anyway. Phocian had found to his delight (as a man he had lived among overly-articulate people) that cows didn't need to talk at all. A good loud moo covered a multitude of meanings: "I'm hungry. The hired man is coming. It's milking time. The clover is good over here." What else was worth saying?

One large, reddish cow did tell of her experiences with a bull, and Phocian listened with feigned interest. She was the only one in the milk herd that had had a calf by natural means. All the others, including Phocian, owed their brief sex life to the efficient administrations of a veternarian. It appeared that Farmer Willis could not afford to buy a bull, and as he planned to give up the farm soon, for he was quite old, he thought he wouldn't bother about raising any new calves. Many of the milk herd cows had been allowed to run dry.

Phocian, as far as he could tell, had sprung full-grown from the brow of some cow-like Zeus; that is to say, he had no memories of his calf days. No cow in the herd seemed to be his mother, and Phocian thought it in poor taste to make inquiries. Phocian reasoned that he must have been a mother at one time, too, but any memories of his occurrence had completely faded. Phocian wondered, idly, what he would have done if there had been a bull about the place. He would have merely informed the creature that he really was a man and sent him about his business. But then Phocian had remembered seeing a bull once in his mandays; they didn't look as if they would stop to talk about whether or not Phocian truly was a cow. Phocian shuddered at this thought.

When winter came on there were many raw and bitter days spent out of doors, and Phocian often thought that his owners should have put him in the barn. He would stand in the snow and slush then and moo loudly at the farm house, getting as close to the front door as he could.

"I wonder why that brown cow hangs around the house all day," he'd hear Mrs. Willis saying. "Maybe she's lonely since she lost her calf."

But this mournful mooing never got Phocian into the barn except at milking time; thus he huddled with the other cows in the herd, his back to the wind, and the winter days passed somehow. When spring came again Phocian was allowed to dry up and he spent a great deal of the time away from the herd, investigating odd sections of the farm, walking through the willow bushes that lined a small creek, and talking to any birds that chanced by. Phocian found, much to his surprise, that one farflung part of the pasture bordered a strip of well-traveled highway, and he began to stand there hour upon hour and gaze at the cars and trucks whizzing by. They seemed to him now like strange bugs. Then, too, they went much faster than the days when he had been in the human world, and they made less noise—a sibilant whooshing sound that almost lulled Phocian to sleep.

Phocian never seemed to tire of seeing the cars zip past, and often the hired man would be obliged to strike him with a stick to get him to the barn. Many times, too, the hired man being too tired to trudge to the edge of the pasture, he would leave Phocian there and he would spend all night looking, looking at the lights of the cars and listening for their pleasant swooshing sounds. He tried to get a glimpse of the people who drove the cars, but they went by so fast, hunched over the wheels, that Phocian could not see them.

He thought again, during those times spent near the highway, how harried and nervous the drivers of the cars must be, and how nice it was, after all, to be a cow and to let others hurry to work, to meetings...to...to...Where had he gone when he had been human? He'd quite forgotten. No one expected a milk cow to do anything: give milk if she was fresh, chew her cud, stand in the sun. Really quite a good life, all things considered.

But then, after a year or two on the farm, Phocian began to get restless. This was in part due to his neglect, for Farmer Willis no longer seemed to care if Phocian was fresh or if he was warm and had food. Phocian would be allowed to wander the farm at will and he would stare longer and longer at the cars going past. Where on earth were they all going? What were the drivers doing in that other, strange world? Was there a war on again? Who was the new President? How many cylinders did cars have now? Maybe, Phocian began to think, maybe he was missing something by being a cow and just standing endlessly by the highway.

One day, late in summer, Phocian had thought to push down the fence and stop a car. They all went by so fast, and paid no attention to his plaintive mooing. He felt then that he really must find out some news of that other world. Perhaps nothing significant was going on, and then he could go back to chewing his cud in the pasture. Surely old Willis had nothing of note to say on the events of the world. Phocian, indeed, once had mooed at Willis, mentioning the weather and his neglect, and Willis had only kicked him and said, "Son of a bitch, get out of my way!" A crude, ugly man, really, and there could be no communcation with such a clod. Therefore Phocian thought that if he only could stop one of those whizzing little bugs, he perhaps could demand news of world affairs from the occupants.

The more he thought about his plan, the more reasonable it seemed, and so quite calmly Phocian had pushed aside a fence post with his head and stumbled and lumbered out onto the highway. It was getting dusk and the cars were starting to blink on their parking lights. Phocian waited in a barrow pit for a moment, and then singled out a large olive-colored truck.

Of course the truck couldn't stop on such short notice, and then, belatedly, Phocian had realized that no one would much want to talk to a cow about politics or world affairs. "Halt!" said Phocian to the truck. But this had come out, "moo!" The brakes of the truck squealed alarmingly and Phocian had felt a shock of some sort and there was a great deal of blood around someplace, he was sure. "Moo moo," Phocian heard himself bellow after a time, and he meant this to mean: "What is going on in this busy, screwed-up world?" But then, strangely, it had sounded, at least to himself, like his favorite phrase: "abbatoir in the offing."

Next, there was a funny "zippa zippa" noise in Phocian's head; he looked around for his friend the magpie, but a red haze was settling over his eyes. The truck driver and his friends looked down at Phocian lying grotesquely in the barrow pit at the edge of the highway.

"Maybe we'd better shoot the critter, sergeant," a man in an olive drab raincoat said. "She seems to be still suffering."

ON MY BEING DEAD

It all began when I reached in my hip pocket and my car keys weren't there. No, it started earlier than that. I had pulled up at a stop light (on my way to the clinic for a checkup) in the center lane, next to a bus. There, in the window of the bus, was an old, old man, tapping on the window at me, gesturing, with sort of an idiotic smile on his face, his mouth drooling. His head was nodding as if to say: "you, too, will be on this bus from the Happy Farm someday, going to a picnic or some damn thing." *Don't you think you can escape*, he seemed to say, as the light changed (thank God) and I let the bus pull ahead. Then he thumbed his nose at me. I was about to thumb back when I saw, what I had feared, the bus was from the state loony hospital at Okonnee.

Anyway, I was sure it was an evil omen of the deepest dye. And then when my car keys were gone, I began to flip; quietly, that is. Car keys are my security blanket, and so the bottom seemed to drop out of everything. Didn't Faulkner once say Americans love their cars more than their wives? I don't think my Buick was named co-respondent in my recent divorce proceedings, but it could have been. Well, I froze right where I was on the parking strip and sat down. I knew I'd have to reconstruct things, a piece at a time. I would make myself born again; tear myself out of my own un-Zeus-like sweating forehead. But it would take some doing, for how does a dead man drive a car?

I sat on the parking lawn, wondering if it was worthwhile trying to breathe, but slowly I felt in all my pockets and found the car keys; they were in my right-hand pants pocket, not where they belonged. I sensed, vaguely, that I'd have to do one thing at a time or I'd stay frozen on the lawn forever. So I put my little brown key case in front of me and said aloud: this key is for the house, where I'm no longer welcome, this one is for the trunk, and this one for the ignition, and this one for the car doors.

Next, I took each one off their hooks and laid them out in a row. Then I took the car door key and went around to the street side and opened the door. And then I came back to the lawn and laid the door key down next to the others, and picked up the ignition key. Then I shuffled around again and stuck the ignition key in its lock, and by that time I began to get some sort of grip on myself; the world started to spin back into place and I could do two or three things at once again; mainly, shift gears, and watch for traffic, is what I had in mind.

So I went to the parking strip and picked up the rest of the keys and my leather case, and went back to the car and got in slowly, looking at my face in the rear car mirror to see if I was really here. "I'll write an essay," I said to my face in the mirror. "How I went to the doctor's and found I was dead."

My being dead this way got off to this dramatic start just before my divorce, and I went to the clinic for a checkup. I thought maybe my long harangues with the wife were due, in part, to my ill health or nerves or something. I sat then in an inner office, waiting, and fairly soon along came a neat-looking Med Tech nurse who, out of a Chinese box, took a blood-pressure contraption. She felt around for my pulse on my wrist and then switched to my right, all this with a tight little smile on her face. "Hmm, that's funny," she said. "Let's have your left arm again." I obliged. "I do declare," she said. And then she strapped on the rubber gizmo and began to pump up the small black bulb. Nothing happened. No juice ran up the little tube.

"Ah... blood pressure's a little low?" I asked. Nursey smiled. "Well, this machine's on the blink, I guess." In half an hour she came back with a doctor in tow. "I can't handle this one," she whispered to the doc. "No pulse."

The clinic doctor, a grey, pinched-face little man, smiled an indulgent smile that said to me: "well, you know about these underpaid helpers. Can't even shove a rectal thermo up an elephant without two doctors from Mayo." He bustled around, felt for my pulse and his face turned tomato red. "Well, I declare," he said. And then quickly he strapped the mechanism on my left arm and began pumping the bulb. No fluid shot up the tube.

Nursey began to giggle. "According to this, he's dead!"

"Well, I don't feel absolutely dead," I came back, "just a little around the temples."

The doctor laughed. "It could be this machine. Take a walk around the block. I mean, come back tomorrow. We'll take a urine sample, meanwhile."

They sent me in the bathroom with a little jar. But I couldn't go.

The nurse's saying "he's dead" to me was probably responsible for my lack of cooperation. But I'd been feeling dead inside about things with my marriage breaking up and all. And I knew I was just walking around, talking, sitting, standing, acting like one alive. But not, really. And so as I've said, when I got back to my car it really hit me, and the doctor's crack about the machine being out of whack didn't help.

And that's why, after a week or two of hesitation, I went to a mental doc and started this group therapy thing. That's what we do nowadays. In Chaucer's time we would all go on a pilgrimage to Canterbury when things got too sticky. But now we go to group therapy and sit in a circle without a very jolly host to egg us on telling our life stories, but a miserable, wizened-up head shrinker with a hell of a penetrating stare and a sarcastic tongue.

We all sit facing our little leader and ... well, perhaps Chaucer should write this entire affair. I mean, "a Knighte there was" and all that. But to be sure, there are no knights these drear days. And what's worse, no Chaucers. But anyway ...

A fat lady there was in this group—all 350 pounds of her. She did have something in common with the Prioress old Geoffrey wrote about. She was on her way to our modern-day Canterbury, Adjustment City, where the bones of a few of our saints are buried: Freud, maybe some of Menninger's boys, Jung of course. She was on this pilgrimage because she couldn't stop eating. That was obvious. But why she ate so much was hard to get at. But as I say, she reminded one of the Prioress, for she carried snacks and cookies in a large purse, and she was, in truth, a dainty nibbler. No crumb stained her lips or dribbled down her enormous bosom.

There was a miller, too, or rather, a baker. He suffered from *acedia* as near as one could tell. "All those thousands of doughnuts," he would say, tears welling up in his extra-large brown eyes. "All those doughnuts day after day—and what did it mean, after all?" he would ask. We didn't know.

And there was a slim, bitter-looking Wife of Bath type. But a wife with a reverse twist. She worked at a munitions plant, and between husbands she masturbated and took no pains to spare our feelings about this subject; I mean, why, when and how she masturbated. And did this mean she really hated all men? Or what? We couldn't answer her. And the chief therapist was of no help to us, for in group therapy us pots have to heal our own cracks pretty much. It did come out later that the Wife of Bath's first husband got drunk one night and slept with her mother, and this bollixed her up for sure.

Then there was a bald-headed little man who had six kids and none of them would empty the trash bins or drink their orange juice, and every time he beat his kids into some temporary sort of submission, his wife, a Dr. Spock devotee, would sleep with the milkman to get even. And then he would run around with his secretary and wonder in between times if he should get a divorce. But then he was a strict Catholic and didn't quite dare. So we didn't know what to tell him, either.

So, we were a pretty sordid, mixed-up bunch, and we were all pretty much paralyzed in the matter of good sound advice or therapy as it's called. And our host, an old sour-puss Harry Bailey, did not offer much of any prize, except tranquilizer pills, for the one who told the most macabre or fascinating story, but I came pretty close to winning when I tried to tell them all about this strange feeling of being dead most of the time.

In all modesty, I meant to say, I was the only one in the therapy unit remotely resembling Chaucer's knight; although to be sure, I lacked the qualities of *gentillesse* that Geoffrey admired so much. But I claim the right to tell my story ahead of the others, mainly on account of my income was a bit higher, and as a TV performer of sorts, and an instructor in freshman composition at the local junior college, I felt a step higher in the social scale than the baker, the masturbating munitions worker and the fat lady, and the father with six kids. Besides, it must be obvious I know a bit more about myself than the others—and another thing that is painfully obvious: I'm not a Chaucer anyway, and can't peer into anybody's soul except my own.

Now my being dead this way didn't quite start with the divorce proceedings or the visit to the doctor's clinic. There was this earlier difficulty I had at work. To begin somewhere near the beginning, I suppose you might say that student-faculty lunch-rooms at a small junior college shouldn't have mirrors. But despite Sartre's play, my idea of hell *is* a place with mirrors. You are very apt to see yourself as you are, and although you cross your fingers and whisper the fairy tale prayer, there is no pleasant answer. Not when you're skidding into the late forties on a spreading stomach.

I saw this glimpse of myself in the lunchroom mirrors: an unpressed corduroy suit, my necktie askew from the collar and this flabby look; or rather, a flabby-pathetic look. I was scanning the lunchroom for a friendly face and it was empty of such. In fact, these days I often think about what Dickens said to Godfrey Nickleby: *"It is extraordinary how long a man may look among the crowd without discovering the face of a friend, but it is no less true. Mr. Nickleby looked and looked, till his eyes became sore as his heart, but no friend appeared; and when, growing tired of the search he turned his eyes homeward, he saw very little there to relieve his weary vision."* I felt I might as well have been in the Gobi desert. The mirror showed a chubby optimistic face— really, my whole appearance was like a complete ass, or a seedy door-to-door salesman.

I felt I might as well have been in the Gobi desert. The mirror showed a chubby optimistic face—really, my whole appearance was like a complete ass, or a seedy door-to-door salesman.

But then, after this devastating glimpse in the mirror, I managed usually to reconstitute myself quickly. I do this by putting on, so to speak, this philosopher's coat—not one of many colors—but a handy grey drab one that lets you trudge through life without anyone noticing much. I remake myself quite often this way, for I seem some sot of putty that can be kneaded this way and that; not all my fault.

I said a philosopher's coat, but I'm talking about a philosopher friend of mine who, indeed has few friends but much respect in the college philosophy department. He keeps his eyes to the floor and walks through the lunchroom quickly as if on some fairly urgent errand; it's a walk and a set of the head that shows some resignation that there will, in all likelihood, be no friendly face to beckon to him to a table. And when things are going badly with me, which seems about every day now, I assume his shape, or at least his head-down walk, and I get through the day.

But of course, he has the advantage; he looks like a philosopher, head down, lost in thought: a complete entity unto himself. Centuries ago, according to Plato or somebody, we were all a solid unit of a man-woman combo; we needed no one else. Well, my friend I speak of, has somehow molded himself into this being, and it has set. But as I say, I am of putty. I need a smile, a wave of the hand now and then or I start to come unglued. I need to be, if not exactly well-liked, at least waved at. I need a lunch-room companion and a welcoming glance—two things rare in this Sahara of mine; not all my fault, either.

The point in question here is: how did I get in this putty condition? My very unpressed clothes proclaim a lack of starch. Not too admirable to be rigid, I suppose, but Lord, it gets you through the day without melting down into this bubble-gum concoction, this *Unidentified Floating Object* which I have become.

Maybe it was my religion; or I mean, the lack of it, that pushed me into this putty mixture. My father started out fairly hard-core Jewish; there was a rabbi in his background somewhere. He married my mother, Lisa, who was of German Catholic background. Why these two got together, I don't know. Propinquity, convenience, lack of choice in a small Western town for my mother; who knows about such things? Anyway, father felt mildly obligated to send me to a temple, which being decided, I went obediently, being mostly putty from the start.

Then mother said I should at least go to a Catholic school, if not the church, out of respect to her own "sainted mother" to balance things out. I, at some dingy parochial school, bowed sheepishly before a wooden cross each class day. Then, father got mad at Temple elders; he had donated a small sum to rebuilding the Sunday school, and the elders gave him a seat behind a pillar. Sulking, he joined the Unitarian church. I went there each Sunday with him and heard, as I recall, mostly book reviews.

So you can see what I mean about a mixed-up, fluid family life. Next, came the Depression and my love of music, hand in hand. Bach wrote for the Christian church; Bach was my first, putty-like love. To get near Bach, I sang in a Lutheran choir.

Then, I suppose hard times had much to do with it all. We couldn't afford a record player or a piano, or I might have gotten Bach out of my system that way. And then, due to the Depression, my family went first to the Temple for financial aid, jobs and whatnot. We got nothing but kind words. An unsuccessful Jew loses status immediately—especially an unsuccessful, Unitarian-type Jew. But the Lutheran church said yes, to me at least. It raised my salary in the choir, and let me do janitor work, and so my putty soul said nuts to the Jewish faith, and hooray for Christian charity. But I didn't quite mean this; visions of Abraham and Moses, their arms raised in wrath against me, rose often in my eyes.

Later on, I went to college and had a crash-collision course with the scientific method. And then I threw up my hands about all faiths—all but Johann Bach; he was all right. What I'm trying to say is that I do believe a firm stance taken when one is a mere child helps to mold character. Thus at the age of 40 or so when you get one of those crushing glimpses of yourself in a mirror, you really don't start to crumble so and slop over the edges in this shameful manner.

We putty types then, when asked firmly: what is your religion? We wilt. For with one memory cell tuned to the Nazi gas chambers we're not too sure it's a good idea to admit having Jewish blood.

"Look," we answer when asked about religious faith, "when you ask about my religion are you genuinely interested in the state of my soul, or just curious?" And right away the asker's attention begins to wander; they don't really want a long boring story of how my father was made to sit behind a pillar and went to the Unitarian church out of spite, or pique.

And then their eyes search out a spot on your pants, or the way your collar button is undone because it's too hot to keep tight shut like the people who are molded right can, no matter what the temperature.

And of course, sooner or later, when you're a putty man, you bollix up in your work. On top of this insignificant post I had in the English department at an insignificant junior college, I had to moonlight. They don't pay junior college instructors enough to keep them half alive, so I got me a kooky job in TV. I was one of those people forever lurking on the fringes of show business. I do have a sensitive face; all of us putty types do. And yet, I'm not quite handsome enough, over-all, to break into TV drama. So the television ad agency people found my proper niche. I became one of the small army hired by the ad agencies to try, with much lip-smacking, eye-rolling, and mmm-saying, to plug thereby a gooey substitute for whip cream and the like.

We were coached (by a frustrated drama director) upon first tasting the product, to look skeptical, then shift over quickly to surprise, and then with consummate grace, switch our facial expression over to utter delight. Sometimes we would drink a brand of coffee before the cameras and a look of revelation was supposed to come over our phiz; you know, as if we had discovered the Holy Grail or something of a like order. And usually I was pretty good at this with my putty face and expressive eyes and all. And the money was surprisingly good in this stupid racket. A racket, by the way, that could take place only in a country obsessed with keeping up a gross national product figure.

But as I say, we putty types end up bad. One bad day our TV gang had to do an ad about whip cream—live and not on tape. And instead of looking pleased about the new whip cream substitute my TV wife was forcing down my throat, I threw up on camera. Sort of throwing up my whole silly life, if you know what I mean. But how could I explain this to the ad agency? So I was instant-fired. To this day, I'm proud to say, the whip cream concoction doesn't sell very well.

But worse still when you're a putty man you come a cropper in your marriage, for about all women are Chaucer's Wife of Bath people and they love to domineer and mold silly men. And when they get their hands into a mess of sticky putty, Lord knows what will come out. You get shaped first this way, then that. Like a woman arranging and rearranging her furniture in the front room. Pretty soon, of course, the hand on the potter's wheel slips and all they've got is a blob, a glob of some mixture. And this doesn't suit them, either.

And it all ends up with a box on the ear for somebody, or crockery throwing, and a door slam that heralds still another *Doll's House* sort of ending, but in reverse. And next thing you know you're in a small bachelor apartment, stunned, stupified, not getting to see your children much, watching TV, eating TV dinners, and taking endless pills because your stomach gets all twisted up in the process somewhere along this long, long line.

What line, you may ask? This long, long trolley ride on the way to our current Canterbury, where only the smug saints who have molded their characters into something firm, into something that can be caught in the mirror and crack the damn glass, make it to the saint's tomb. Or rather, as I say, to Adjustment City—damn its black heart to hell.

Well, to be sure, our leader, this ersatz Harry Bailey, invited us all to a picnic one summer day as part of his therapy where we would all get to know each other better, or so he said. Of course, the hospital had a Funny Farm bus. I sat by the window, planning to make faces at the lucky people in private cars when we stopped for traffic lights.

But the Wife of Bath, plunked herself down next to me, and I thought to myself, I'd be a sight better than masturbation for her. So I thought I'd put the make on her at the picnic. What did I have to lose, after all? What did she have to lose? So full speed ahead, I said to her, and damn the hot dogs and mustard. And she smiled at me, her first warm smile in two years, I bet.

Photo Credit: Dr. Jean Wyrich

L.W. Michaelson was born in Denver, Colorado in 1920. He earned degrees from The University of Arizona, The University of Iowa Writers' Workshop, and The University of Denver. At present, he is an assistant professor at Colorado State University where he teaches creative writing, science fiction, and American literature.